Ann Tracy was born in Bangor, Maine, and studied at the University of Toronto. She now divides her time between Toronto and Plattsburg where she teaches English at the State University of New York. A specialist in eighteenth-century literature, she has published two major studies of the gothic novel, *Patterns of Fear in the Gothic Novel* (1980) and *The Gothic Novel: 1790–1830* (1981). Several of her short stories have appeared in anthologies. *Winter Hunger* is her first novel.

WINTER HUNGER

ANN TRACY

Published by VIRAGO PRESS Limited April 1993
20–23 Mandela Street, Camden Town, London NW1 0HQ

First published in Canada by Goose Lane Editions 1990

Excerpts from Morton I. Teicher's "Windigo Psychosis" reproduced
by permission of the American Anthropological Association from *American
Ethnological Society Proceedings* of the 1960 Annual Spring Meeting.
Not for further reproduction.

A CIP catalogue record for this book is available from the British Library

Printed in Great Britain by Cox & Wyman Ltd, Reading, Berkshire

For Bill and Michelle,
who made Wino Day possible

Early in November, when winter seemed already to have been at Wino Day Lake forever, Alan began to dream about Proxene Ratfat. Or, to be more precise, he told himself as he lay gingerly under the quilt, about her vile drawings. He opened his eyes so that he could stop seeing the picture, but it floated defiantly on the murk of the northern morning before it faded. In his dream he had been skating on white drawing paper that lay stretched like the icy lake outside his trailer, skating better than he'd ever been able, and wielding a broom with which he was trying to curl her ugly little designs right off the edge of the paper rink. The things were as heavy as real curling stones and they had, besides, a tendency to snap at his skates, for all Proxene's loony-colored critters, her crazed paisley patterns, her crazlies, had little fanged edgings like rickrack gone bad. Neither in his dream nor in life did her pictures, patterned or strewn over the paper, make representational sense to him, though now and then a form would suggest itself – here a mosquito, there a vulva, occasionally a fish. He'd never yet seen a Ratfat that didn't claw his nerve endings, and there was at least one tacked up in every kitchen in town except his. Smelly old Proxene would just roll up and hand them out like summonses or shove them under the door, and the women, always the women, would tack them up.

Women, he thought, woman, and let his left hand drift a little closer to the warmth of his sleeping wife. He inhaled the hot domestic odor of her sleep and traces of the fern soap that she'd hauled with her into the wilderness. That side felt good. He inched his right hand more cautiously toward the unprotected side of the bed and out into the air. It was cold out there, but no crazlies sank their tiny purple fangs into his fingers. Perhaps it would do to get up. Impossible to tell from the darkness whether it was four a.m. or eight. Could he indeed get up now and avoid the risk of further dreams? He raised himself on one elbow, staying inside the blankets, and peered at the alarm clock on the far side of his wife. Five fifteen. Or was it three twenty-five? He squinted again, remembering the time he'd gotten up, back in Michigan, and eaten breakfast at half past midnight, mistaking it for six o'clock in the morning. He'd been really worried that it was so dark, suspecting the end of the world, but he was going to have breakfast anyway.

No, he had it right this time. It really was five fifteen. Early, but possible. Cam, their baby, was still blessedly silent in his curtained cubicle. At sixteen months he was beginning to sleep a little later, thank God.

Four years of marriage had made him adept at sliding out of bed without joggling the mattress. He looked with longing at his wife's shoulder and the back of her neck, wanting to kiss them, even just to touch them with the tip of his tongue before he got up, but discretion prevailed. Diana slept lightly towards morning.

In yesterday's jeans and grey sweater, which he had

scooped off the floor on his way to the kitchen, he padded to the propane stove and set a saucepan of water to boil while he sourly considered his environment, not for the first time. Though he was living in what should have been an anthropologist's dream – isolation, a town full of Indians, and not another social scientist in sight – he was not having fun. He was having, instead, native-flavored nightmares. Alan poured part of the water into a mug with a spoonful of instant coffee, set some water aside on another burner for Diana, and threw two handsful of oatmeal into the rest, clinging to the remnants of his conviction that hot cereal in the morning and sub-arctic isolation equalled coziness for the nuclear family.

Carrying his coffee to the oilcloth-covered table by the window, still groggy and tasting the staleness of his unbrushed teeth with a kind of unfocused resentment, he let his mind mumble on. Wino Day Lake. He had picked it out by chance on a map of northern Manitoba, a perfectly suitable Indian community, and the name had tickled him. It reminded him of his father.

Actually, the natives said with some contempt that the name was wrong on the white man's maps, that it was (variously) Wine Dago Lake or Wet Dago Lake, or that was what it sounded like, though it didn't make much sense. He'd never seen it spelled. The random whites in the community, the Hudson Bay boys, the nurses, the teachers, the young brother on the mission staff, liked to amuse themselves at parties by inventing stories about the town's naming, all variations on the theme of drunken Italian visitors or explorers or trappers falling into the lake or otherwise coming to damp ends. Alan didn't find the stories very amusing any more, if he ever had. He didn't find the place very amusing.

As for cozy, cozy had two faces. The tight feeling that he and Diana and Cam were together against the world had been good at first, was very often still good. But sometimes when he thought about the high skies of his midwestern childhood and looked up at the low grey skies of northern Canada – looked across at them maybe, or even down at them as they just cleared the tops of the stunted trees – he imagined a universe that looked like a schematic rendering of the human eyeball, with the colored circle of the iris the round earth and the white the surrounding sky. And he was a creature who had started life on one of earth's side places where the sky stretched forever, and his life had been spent crawling up to the top places where the sky was so low there wasn't room to stand up straight. It snowed there too, in a boring, relentless way, and his alternative image of Wino Day was that if he should get on top of his roof and stick his hand straight up he could touch the glass of his sno-globe prison.

He scratched the base of his skull, tangling his fingers in his hair, which would stand out in snarly bushes until he combed it down, and tried to think about his day's work. Riddle: what's more work than working? His bloody damned dissertation. "Kin Networks and Food Jurisdiction in Three Communities" – he recited the title to himself with distaste. What the hell kind of topic was that anyway, he had begun to wonder. It sounded silly up here, even though (or perhaps because) it was about places not unlike this. Somehow real Indians distracted one from Indian statistics, and it was more fun to pull fish nets in one community than to write about food jurisdiction in three. But the dreary thing was progressing, however slowly, and it looked as though he would have a draft finished in late spring, thanks to Wino Day's isolation and a timely legacy from Diana's Aunt Ida, who had raised her.

He tried, as always when he thought of Aunt Ida, to imagine Diana as a child. The idea was oddly titillating. Not that he was a pervert; he wasn't. Children didn't turn him on sexually or any other way. But Diana as a child – if Diana were a child, pigtailed, overalled, sticky with sweat and lollipop, well then he would be omnipotent to her, able to kiss her scabby elbows better or make her day with an ice cream cone. Unsolicited film clips of Diana's childhood, elaborations on family snapshots, flickered through his head as he heaved his body up and dumped some oatmeal into a bowl, adding canned butter and brown sugar to the top. It made an unappealing mess, but there was no fresh milk and he hated powdered.

He still adored his wife. Adoring her, he let himself slide into a familiar someday fantasy. Someday he'd have his degree and be Dr. Hooper; and maybe, God willing and the wind in the right direction, Professor Hooper in spite of the declining academic job market. Professor Hooper and his beautiful wife, with an oriental rug in the living room and *The New York Times* on the doorstep and a patio with sunshine all around. Someday telephones again, colored, with push buttons. Two cars, ecologically sound but sporty. Roads, real roads with white stripes down the black middles, to drive them on. Professor Hooper with fresh fruit on his cereal, fresh butter on his toast, sometimes even cream in his coffee. Professor Hooper, distinguished anthropologist, with faceless students begging to help with his field work and type his notes.

The hypothetical Professor Hooper's future wife, Alan Hooper's wife Diana, beautiful by God right now without an oriental rug to her name, stood in the doorway to the kitchen in her old yellow bathrobe, a garment as dearly familiar to him as the curve of her shoulder beneath it. She pushed back her straight dark hair with her left hand, using her right to balance the fat, soaking, sleep-creased burden on her right hip. Alan contemplated his fussy son with revulsion. Involuntary, of course. Reminding himself that he was none too attractive in the morning either, Alan strove for some impulse of parental affection. Sometimes he could get it (not very often, if he was to be honest about it), but he could find this morning nothing but a twinge of resentment. Not jealousy. But if he were as filthy and fractious as the baby, she wouldn't press him to her body, would she? Hardly. Why not carry the little beast by his armpits, or make him walk; he knew how when he wanted to. The casual intimacy of Cam's body on Diana's hip set his teeth on edge. She was too good for it – impeccable, lovely Diana, his queen and huntress forever, though virgin no longer.

Cam was a sour note in their harmony, no getting around that, but almost the only one. Almost. The other nagged at the back of Alan's mind from time to time, but it didn't howl and piss and rattle the bars of its crib, so he could ignore it better than he could ignore Cam: Diana was working on a book. Diana, with her bare B.A., was compiling data on women's indigenous art for a book that looked as though it might sell, while he, Alan, king and breadwinner, was still trapped in his dissertation, first book waiting somewhere off in oriental-rug land. Proxene's drawings weren't on his kitchen wall because they were, in fact, in a file folder under Cam's crib.

Diana spared him an amiable look on her way to the bathroom – it was their custom to preserve decency with a few minutes of silence while they first pulled themselves together – and closed the door on Cam's cries. When they emerged again, Cam clean and rosy and better-natured, Diana even more fetching after some subtle reorganization with soap and comb, he had poured coffee into a second mug and spooned oatmeal into Cam's blue bowl.

"Working today?" Diana asked him as she kissed him on the forehead and sat down across from him with Cam on her lap. Though he suspected that the question was mere rhetorical pleasantry, he wished that she wouldn't ask it. A sensitive topic, one's dissertation. A perpetual twinging burden that sat on the shoulders like a hump. He always imagined it to look like Christian's burden of sins in the

Blake illustrations to *Pilgrim's Progress*, a muscular lump grown right to his back, made of the same stuff as his flesh. On the day that it tumbled off, he asked himself, would he remember how to stand up straight?

Perceiving that his "Yes" had been surly, he cleared his throat and tried again. "I'm pretty well through the third chapter," he said, for he did want to be agreeable in response to his wife's undoubted good will. "If I put in four hours this afternoon, I should be able to fool around tonight." They had the whole winter (O God, the whole winter) and spring, such as it would be, so there was no need to push himself if he worked nearly every day. He'd probably do less than four hours, in fact; at best four hours broken up by coffee and runaway fantasies and fruitless pseudo-errands around the house, but a man's intentions might as well exceed his grasp.

"I'd like to go to Naomi's," she said. "I think Cam will take a nap right after lunch. I had to leave in the middle of a good conversation yesterday."

Cam seized the opportunity, as she looked up, to drop his spoon and thrust his hand into his oatmeal. The brief hiatus while Diana held Cam's hand under the tap, dried it on a dishtowel, and came back to her chair gave Alan time to organize himself for magnanimity. Of course he preferred Diana by his side, but he admitted that Naomi was good for her.

"Sure," he said. "If Cam wakes up I'll put some toys in his crib. We'll be fine."

Alan got on well enough with the local men, but he knew that Diana and Naomi had something special. Diana missed the mother she could barely remember and now she missed her aunt besides, and somehow the old Indian woman with her proud, halting English took the edge off her loss. Moreover, with Naomi Diana could immerse herself in native handicrafts, learning the subtleties of patterns and beading and furs. She'd come home muttering happily about Miriam Shapiro and the apotheosis of feminine fabric art, and make notes in the bedroom before she'd come out to talk with him or play with Cam. She had a special kind of happy look, too, when she came back, that might be creative inspiration or might be the effect of Naomi's leathery mothering and cups of tea. Of course, he told himself, she couldn't be expected to spin all that maternal stuff for Cam out of nothing; she must need some input too. His anthropologist's mind noted with idle interest that the instinct to form chains of nurturing was strong enough to cross cultures.

Diana shoved the last of the cereal into Cam's mouth, scraped his lower lip, and tried to drink some of her cooling coffee, fending off her son's inquisitive hand. "It's funny," she said. "I'm not the anthropologist in this outfit, but when I'm with Naomi I feel absolutely at home. I mean, you wouldn't think we come from different worlds. We hardly even need language, and to tell the truth I like it better when Sarazine isn't hanging around to translate, even if she is Naomi's granddaughter. Naomi is just so *quick*."

Inwardly Alan sighed a little, for he was used to recitations of Naomi's virtues – tough, bright, kind, clever with her hands, outrageously witty. He could recite them himself. Diana was seeing her now almost every day. Female bonding always made him cross – why couldn't men talk to each other? it wasn't fair – but mainly he felt out-anthropologized: how come it was always his wife who could get close to the natives? She didn't seem to feel the barriers that made him shy, perhaps because she was so much her own person that she was not greatly bound to the habits and biases of her own culture. The only compensation was that sometimes she brought home pieces of information useful to his work. He'd never known Diana to get close to someone as fast as this, but as it was only for a year it didn't matter. He was still the lead dog and he was planning to head south. Swept by possessive pity, thinking how sad his wife would be at losing yet another maternal figure, he resolved to make it up to her.

Cam was beginning to bleat insistently and tug at Diana's robe. "Meh!" he cried, having lately achieved some consonants but nothing further. His speech was ugly but interesting. Alan and Diana would guess what he wanted while he belched M's – "More? Mommy? Milk?" Sometimes they would guess wild – "Monkey wrench? Miracle play? Motorcycle?" It drove Cam crazy. M usually stood for Mommy or milk, in fact, and perhaps there was no distinction to be made there, Alan thought ruefully as Diana unveiled one glorious breast to Cam's oatmealy mouth. Oh yes indeed, he was a breast man, he thought, keeping himself to his own side of the table with an effort. BC, as he liked to think of that idyllic period, Before Cam, they often used to go straight back to bed after breakfast if the notion took them, and it frequently did. Well, they'd been to bed once too often, that was all, he thought as he looked at Cam, but then he felt dreadfully guilty. He didn't mean that, of course.

Cam and Diana actually made a very pretty picture, what with Cam's pink cheeks and Diana's yellow robe and the way her hair fell down as she bent over him. His very own 3-D madonna and child. Sharply protective at first when Diana had insisted on nursing beyond the usual period, and stung by a collection of other emotions that he had refused to examine or classify, he had protested that Cam would get teeth and bite, that Cam's character would be ruined, and (absurdly) that Cam wouldn't appreciate it. Now he was obliged to admit that Cam seemed disinclined to bite or give way to moral decay. His gratitude, presumably, was appropriate to his age and inexperience – minimal. But Alan himself had brought them away from cows and dairies, to the north where they would rely upon one another, and there was no disputing Diana's gastro-

nomical superiority to powdered milk. For a moment he
felt all the warmth and domestic felicity that he had imagined the long winter's closeness would bring about.

Party invitations were not easily come by in Wino Day, so
Naomi's seventieth birthday party constituted an occasion.
Diana's pleasure was straightforward: she liked a good
time and she adored Naomi. Alan's was rather more complicated. He would have gone to a hanging to get away
from his dissertation for an evening; he had an anthropological yen for further social intercourse with the native
population; and he was, in some measure, lonely.

It was not a significant loneliness, he told himself, for
Diana was the only person he'd ever cared much about.
But in a vague way he missed the warmth of congenial
groups, something he had never consciously valued when
he had it, least of all since his marriage. At least when he
was still in Toronto he could go off to a bar with friends if
he wanted, never mind that he seldom did. Here he had
no friends. He had anticipated that the Indians would
keep him at a certain distance. He had not guessed that
the whites would be miffed at his renting Indian housing;
they weren't unkind exactly, just – again – standoffish.

Neither culture would quite have him. Diana was his passport tonight.

Diana was looking beautiful. She'd put on a modified version of her city clothes for Naomi's party, long black wool skirt, emerald turtleneck sweater. The sight of her shortened his breath. He hadn't seen her dressed up for months.

"What are you staring at, dummy?" she asked him smugly, provocative wench, pinching his stomach and causing him to miss a buttonhole. "Forget it," she added, assessing her effect. "The baby sitter'll be here any minute. Listen, are you *sure* eight is old enough to take care of Cam?"

Alan repeated his assurances that eight-year-old girls, as a cross-cultural phenomenon, are the most reliable of all sitters, keen to emulate their mothers and big enough to hoist a baby.

"At least the next-door neighbors are home," Diana said to herself, apparently ignoring him, "and we won't be too far away ourselves."

Ten minutes later, the sitter installed with a box of Oreos and instructed when to run and shriek for help, Alan took Diana's arm for the proprietorial pleasure of the gesture and helped her ceremoniously down the metal steps of the trailer onto the packed snow. The stars were bright, and farther into the center of town they could see dark human figures, some with lights in their hands, moving towards them. Naomi's daughter Elizabeth lived on the near side of the village center. A little embarrassed about the log cabin which her parents had refused to give up, she was holding the party in her own government-issue house. Laughter and the barking of dogs drifted down along the lake shore. Alan remembered something that at home they called "the holiday season." This felt like the start of it.

Most of Wino Day lay to the north of Alan and Diana's

trailer, where three rows of houses stood parallel to the water. Facing the houses and backing onto the lake itself were the public buildings – the school, the mission church, the priest's house, the post office, the Bay store – and a few private houses whose owners had settled near the water early and weren't budging, for the closer the water, the less labor to carry it. Whites lived on the edges of the town center, and farther out yet were a scattering of assorted dwellings that didn't fit the patterns. Their own fifties trailer to the south, hauled in once upon a time on a barge and set up near the shore, was one. Naomi's cabin to the north was another. Someday, Alan told himself as they crunched along the snow, they would recall this night's partying as a time of youth and unorthodox glamor. In the meantime, it might or might not be comfortable, but he'd hope for the best.

When they reached the door, Elizabeth's grown daughter Sarazine had just opened it to a crowd of well-wishers bearing mysterious parcels for Naomi and less mysterious bottles for their own consumption. "We didn't bring a bottle," Alan hissed to Diana, panicking. With a sidelong flicker of her cool eyes she acknowledged him, reached into her parka pocket with thumb and forefinger, and exposed the top of their silver travel flask. Astounding woman, Diana. She thought of everything.

To their left, as they came into the front hall, they could see a superfluity of women jostling and laughing in the kitchen. Between their shoulders, on the sideboard, Alan could catch glimpses of what looked like a most remarkable monstrous pink cake. They seemed to be teasing Elizabeth's sister about having brought it on a snowmobile earlier that day. It would require a snowmobile at least, Alan thought as he and Diana shed their coats and moved into the living room, maybe even a boxcar. A new angle of vision from the living room into the kitchen suggested that the cake was a good three feet long by two wide, with a round two-layer increment of cake on the center top suggesting either a gun turret or a screw-off cap. The whole effect was made livelier by pink frosting, very bright, and pink sparkles.

He averted his eyes, not quite quickly enough, from what looked to be a new Proxene Ratfat picture tacked to the cupboard door. This one was executed in black and red crayon on an irregular bit of cardboard – Proxene's materials varied by happenstance – and seemed to involve a lot of big toothy somethings chasing a lot of little ones. Alan didn't think that further perusal would make it more pleasant. Proxene herself would at any rate not be at the party; despite a tolerant solidarity among the women, she was beyond the most generous social pale on occasions given to joy, dignity, and physical proximity.

Farther south, in the cities, Proxene would have been a bag lady, Alan supposed. She would have picked trash cans and lurked down subway holes, watching violence and death with her round, inscrutable face. In Wino Day, though, old women were taken care of, and though she belonged to nobody, she belonged to everybody. If nobody was the better for her, nevertheless she was there, and the townspeople shrugged and made the best of it. Like the cold, she was part of their lives. Not even the hunters who brought her fish and bits of caribou, nor the women who brought her their castoffs, could identify the decaying substances with which she had padded her hovel, and it was said that she added new garments to her surface as the old ones rotted away underneath. And bubbling to the top of this compost came the bizarre and unnerving little drawings that Diana was taking seriously as material for her book.

In the living room, Naomi sat on the sofa, a little shy at the formality of the occasion but nonetheless beaming irrepressibly from time to time. Diana joined the group around her while Alan hunkered against the wall, closer to, but not quite with, a knot of men. He thumbed the silver flask that Diana had put into his hands when she took off her parka. It all at once seemed to him damningly sissy, but he unscrewed the top and took a manly pull of the vodka that was all they had on hand. Why couldn't they have had something that at least smelled like alcohol? Looking around to see what the other men were drinking, he realized that his gesture had been premature, possibly even impolite.

Willy Powderhorn leaned over and gave him an encouraging thump on the shoulder, innate good manners covering the outsider's gaffe. "Fast man," Willie said to the others. "He plays the game this spring!" The other men haw-hawed and shoved each other in appreciation. What game? Visions of scapegoats and vegetation rituals raised Alan's uneasiness a level higher. Anthropologists have fuel for very bad dreams.

"Game?" Alan asked weakly, tentative smile on lips.

"Ask Baptiste," offered a short man Alan didn't recognize. "You know him – got one ear!"

Gales of laughter greeted the ear reference. "Got one ear!" a couple of the men said to each other in glee. Baptiste himself, one of whose ears was indeed curiously formed at the top, almost truncated, came into the room just then with his wife.

"Tell this man about the game, Baptiste," someone suggested. Baptiste's wife rolled her eyes at the women and pursed her lips as if to say Men, for god's sake.

"Tell him yourself," Baptiste ventured, embarrassed but good natured. "Guess you remember more." This was clearly a witticism. Alan looked to Diana for help, but Naomi had just said something witty too, and Diana's circle was caught up in its own merriment.

After reminiscent mumbles and chuckles had given Alan time for recovery (after all, Baptiste had at any rate played the game and lived, but would Diana like her own husband without both his ears intact?), Willie offered a terse and perhaps characteristically Indian explanation. "Spring game," he said, grinning. "Everybody feels good, everybody drinks. First man falls down, we shave his head. Everybody not shave too good then. Man wears hat for a while."

"Sound like a good game," Alan said, "ha ha. Guess I'd better get a big hat before spring." This sally made such a hit that his spirits rose, though already he was secretly plotting excuses.

He passed the flask to Diana, now that he saw refreshments coming in and bottles of whiskey coming out. The women looked at the flask with greater favor and one or two of them stroked it. Alan loved to watch his wife tip the flask up and drink from it. The gesture was so full of grace yet at the same time so unfeminine that he felt a slightly perverse excitement, as though he were planning to take some chancy androgynous creature home to bed with him after the party. Out of the corner of his eye he glanced at the men to see if they were admiring her, but their dark faces were inscrutably calm. Perhaps they hadn't even noticed.

Looking down, he found steaming in front of him a dish of some hot, brown, rich-smelling substance. He had seen it before, a staple of local festivities. La Pudden. One usually ate it with canned milk over the top. Diana, who had the recipe from Naomi, speculated that it was the offspring of an early French Christmas pudding. Tonight it appeared in its gala version – they were pulling out all the stops for Naomi – with a homemade syrupy sauce. The stuff was, in fact, pretty good, though funny with vodka. He presumed that it was even funnier with rye, which most of the party seemed to be drinking. Still, one never knew; he had gotten through some tough study sessions in his Toronto apartment with the aid of peanut butter sandwiches and scotch.

The pink extravaganza appeared from the kitchen, and Elizabeth cut and dealt it out. The menu all made sense in frigid Wino Day – lots of sugar, hot pudding instead of cold ice cream. Alan, cake in hand, sidled nearer to Diana, his insides beginning to relax after the game scare. Games. Soon the men would probably be getting out decks of cards and cribbage boards. He didn't want to play anything. He wanted to observe. He wanted to be closer to his madly attractive wife. He hitched his rump across the floor and pushed his right shoulder against her back. "How you doing?" he breathed in the back of her neck.

She leaned back against him a little and passed him the flask. "Fine," she said, keeping her attention on Naomi and her appreciative coterie.

The old woman was in the midst of a story that she rendered into English for Diana's sake. The others knew it anyway; it was a comfortable old favorite. "So Jake say, 'Go take some then; not *my* fish net.' But you know what? *Was* his fish net. Stole from him winter before! His fish net all time!"

Diana laughed as gleefully as the other women. Genuinely, too, Alan realized. They were too close as a couple to overlook any false notes. This laughter worried him slightly. He did not, himself, think the story much of a yuk, even supposing a person knew the first few lines. Had Diana somehow gotten inside the trick of Indian humor, that last impenetrable bastion of any culture? To him the story seemed only mildly amusing, ironic on a low level. Was she leaving him behind? He hoped that she was merely tipsy, for she would never be able to clarify the funniness for him. Once he and a friend had spent two days on a camping trip trying to understand a Ukrainian's explanation of why all Ukrainians double up at any allusion to being kicked by ducks. Communication had failed.

Now Naomi's friends were urging her to open her gifts. Some had come without wrapping – two bottles of wine, a large bunch of plastic anemones. Other objects emerged from colored paper: some pale green towels, coffee mugs in several designs, a ghastly but fascinating religious picture in which a bleeding Christ with closed eyes was transfigured by a tilt of one's hand into open-eyed benevolence, blood and thorns wiped away. Alan began to appreciate the warmth and poise that Diana had so often extolled as he watched the old woman make each giver feel herself the donor of the quintessentially perfect gift. He could not decide whether the twinkle in her black eyes as she thanked Dorcas Dantouze for the Jesus picture was amusement or tears of emotion. Diana would know, perhaps. Though he did not, come to think of it, much like the idea that she could read any book but his own.

And speaking of Diana, what had she brought Naomi? He remembered now a parcel the size of a small loaf that had come along with them, but he had earlier been too bowled over by the green sweater to form a question. "What . . . " he began to whisper in Diana's ear, but she nudged him quiet. Naomi had come to her package. Alan could not imagine what it was. Had Diana gone to the Bay to shop and he forgotten it?

It was a box, dark wood with inlaid floral patterns of brass. He flinched a little, for he had been fond of it. It was the box in which Diana had been accustomed to keep her jewelry. They had bought it together one day in Northampton before they were married. Not that it had been a gift from him; Diana had got it with her own money and it was hers to dispose of. It had come from India and wasn't very extravagant, even for a student budget, but it called up pictures of Green Street and yellow leaves and the first intoxication of reciprocal love. He'd have preferred her to spend quite a lot of money on a new gift that carried no memories.

Now Diana was touching Naomi's knee and saying, "That's for your best beading supplies, and to remember me by because it was mine," and those really were the beginnings of tears in Naomi's eyes this time as she patted Diana's cheek with a gesture awkward in its naked affection; and all at once Alan had to go to the washroom worse than he had realized and there was something wrong with his own eyes, so he sprang up and left the room.

He loitered a little behind the closed door, trying to recognize himself in the mirror. He never could when he'd been drinking. He was always plainer, scruffier, than he thought of himself as being, not to mention more salacious looking and somewhat fuzzy around the edges. It was only eleven o'clock but he thought they'd better go home pretty soon, because after all the sitter would need to be taken home to bed. When he came out, Diana was already getting their coats and thanking Elizabeth. She had always had a good sense of dramatic structure; no doubt the moment with Naomi and the gift was the climax of her evening. That was fine with him. The best thing about a party anyway was the bit at the end when he and nobody else cut Diana out of the herd and claimed her and carried her away to their private lair. Public pairing – it always swelled his head. Among other things.

"By the way," Diana said, hooking her padded elbow through his as they steadied themselves against the wind off the lake, "we're borrowing the town cat tomorrow and you're in charge. Not of the mousing, of course, she'll do that herself, but make sure she doesn't get out of the house. There used to be two cats, you know, but one got out and the sled dogs killed her. They always do, so we're on our honor to be careful. Naomi asked me especially to come by tomorrow and talk, so if you don't mind . . . I'll pick up the cat before I go. It would be a treat for Cam, I should think, if you don't mind my leaving him home."

"Fine, great," Alan said. He was feeling his alcohol. Of course he wouldn't let Cam out, it would be a treat for the cat, or was it the other way? Well, probably both. What was occupying his mind, really, was that he was married to a woman with a long skirt and a silver flask who could talk about *the* town cat without any hint that she found a one-cat town (the northern equivalent of a one-horse town?) at all bizarre. Who, he asked himself not for the first time, was supposed to be getting into the native culture here anyway? "Whazziz his name?" he remembered to ask, feeling polite, "and what she like to eat?" He was pleased to think that he'd buggered up his pronouns like a native.

"Mukluk," Diana said, "unless you mean Cam. And unlike Cam, she gets off on powdered milk. Dry. Or so I'm told."

"And," she said as she steered him up the trailer steps to pay the baby sitter, "did you hear them telling the story about the old woman who ate the berry basket? Because you'll love it."

CHAPTER THREE

At exactly nine twenty-five Diana shut the trailer door on Alan, Cam, the town cat, and the dissertation. Mukluk, a big tortoise shell cat with white feet, was used to making house calls. She was not a public cat by design, but as the only cat in town she was much sought after. Her owners, as attached as any other cat lovers, nevertheless yielded her up with her litter box (sand and baking soda in a cut-down carton) for municipal duty. She would be staying overnight.

Cam was, as Diana had expected, delighted. He plunged after Mukluk, grabbing for handsful of tortoise shell fur, chortling with surprise whenever she lashed his face with her tail. Alan reckoned that entertaining Cam wouldn't be much problem.

He sat down at the kitchen table with his pad of lined paper, his three pens, and a stack of note cards about four inches thick. It was light outside now, and attuned to the hopeful feeling of dawns, even late northern dawns, he plunged in where he had left off the day before and produced three quarters of a page in fifteen minutes. "Fast work, Alan," he congratulated himself, feeling a surge of creative joy. Half an hour later, having written no more than the other quarter page (most of it), he found himself beset by a certain restlessness. An obligation to check on Mukluk's progress began to weigh on him. He found the cat asleep on his quilt and Cam chewing on Diana's moccasin, which had been under the bed. His efforts to take away the moccasin for drying provoked such an outcry that he gave them up.

Back at the table he read the same note card three times and sighed heavily. His notes suggested to him no further strategy of composition. Perhaps, he thought, he could substitute a cookie for the moccasin. Standing up made him feel better all over; he seemed even to breathe more freely. The cookie trade was successful, but it caused the cat, awake again and sniffing encouragingly behind the bureau, to leave its work and show a sudden deceitful interest in Cam.

In the kitchen Alan forced his feet toward the table and then, thinking of powdered milk, veered away to the cupboard just in time before the note cards got him. Whistling to himself, he poured a quarter cup into a saucer. He was rewarded by the sight of a happy cat snorting up the powder, sneezing, licking her chops for leftovers, and purring back to work. Would it make her less hungry for mouse? Or did cats hunt for the pure sport of it? Alan felt inclined to dwell on the question. Cam meanwhile, loving the show, had tried to wash his own face with his paw and now had cookie in his ear, a circumstance that seemed to his father to warrant slow attention with a wet towel.

At the table again, Alan gritted his teeth and bent his head to his notes. How in the seven circles of hell could he ever have thought this stuff interesting? Boring, awful, pedantic folly, that's what it was. But it was a ticket to the good life if he had the discipline to grit through it all. The seven labors of Hercules. Hercules in the Augean stables shoveled less shit than this. And then there was that man in Judaic mythology who worked seven years to get his wife and got the wrong one and had to work another seven: Jacob. Had Jacob found the good life worth the price? Ah, Diana would be worth seventy years of labor, but he already had her and couldn't even enjoy her for this mindless grind. Why did society insist that he sit on a hard chair and make funny marks on lined paper? Well, not society then, it was his own choice. Perhaps if he pretended he was doing this to win Diana, that he didn't have her already —

For as much as five minutes he felt a kind of delusive if unproductive enthusiasm, but before he got anything on paper the thought of Diana took over and ten minutes later, startled by a shriek from Cam, he found himself in a glassy-eyed erotic reverie with one hand clutching his crotch. Just as well that Cam had yelled, he told himself, going to the bedroom to see what was wrong. A fat pink scratch on Cam's hand suggested that he had committed some indiscretion with the cat. Alan carried him by the armpits out to the kitchen, buttered his scratch, and sat him down with some measuring spoons where he could supervise any further social intercourse. He felt wretchedly sleepy. Coffee, he said to himself.

The activity of putting the water on to boil was a relief. Was it really only ten to eleven? Or, alternatively, was his working time so nearly gone? He thawed a hole in the frost-covered window in the kitchen door while the water heated. Finding pen still in hand, he made circles by pressing the eraser end into the frost. He began to poke with more interest, making a round-eyed face surrounded by what he decided must be hair curlers. "Cam," he said, to justify his childish vagary, "see the funny lady." Cam looked at Alan's own face with passing interest but ignored

the pattern of dots in the frost; he went back to chewing
his spoons and beating them on the floor.

Alan absentmindedly added a fanged fringe to the out-
line, started a little at the Ratfatish effect, and melted the
no-so-funny lady with hot, nervous huffings. The lake, re-
vealed through the melted hole, was white as a blank page.
For several reasons, an unfortunate image. Lines of dark
spruce on the nearest island broke the horizon. Two little
boys came into sight carrying five-gallon pails in each
hand. Could such shrimpy kids really carry home those
pails heavy with water? Alan watched. It seemed that they
could. Why, after all, should he doubt it? He had seen
women hauling water in industrial paint buckets, and even
now some man he couldn't identify was coming to the
hole in the ice with two large garbage cans on a sled. He'd
fill them too. Most of the women washed for big families.

He turned back to his coffee water just in time to find
Cam burrowing in the litter box, which the cat had, for-
tunately, so far not used. Or at least he didn't think she
had. Turning off the burner, he flipped his son upside
down over the box and dusted most of the sand and soda
out of his hair. He replaced the measuring spoons with a
real toy, a wonderful little local artifact, two pieces of wood
nailed together in the clear semblance of a snowmobile.
Cam had fallen in love with it at the Dantouze house one
day and the Dantouzes had let him take it home. Their
children were too old for it now. Diana longed to preserve
it as folk art but hadn't the heart to deprive Cam.

Coffee. Table. Pen and paper. But Hercules, come to
think of it, had re-directed a river to run through the
stables and done the job all at once. This was just the opposite. Diana sometimes quoted from a poem about
measuring out your life in coffee spoons. He was measuring out the bullshit in coffee spoons, and a dissertation is
a lot of spoonsful. Before he knew it he was on his feet
again and seeking distraction at the window.

Thank God, someone was setting a fish net under the ice. Surely it behooved him as an anthropologist to watch the process, though he'd seen it once before. He hadn't noticed them chiseling the holes, but there they were with boards and ropes and nets, colorful little figures twenty-five yards out from shore. The ice had to be five feet thick and the snow another couple of feet on top of that. Nature, however, was no bar to human ingenuity. Alan still couldn't figure out the whole process. It was like watching a magic show, or like watching the Indians' hand game when they gambled with sticks, which he couldn't follow either. The men were dropping a long plank down the first hole, he could see that, and it had ropes on it. Somehow, with the ropes, they "walked" it under the ice, that's what they called it, and Willie swore they could hear exactly where it was. And then, like a rabbit out of a hat, the damned thing finally popped up the other side and it had the fish net with it and there they were, net all set and accessible. It drove him crazy not to know how they managed at the end, but the only time he'd asked they'd acted as though he were joking, so he'd had to pretend that he was and he didn't see how he could ask again.

Finishing his coffee, he cast a glance at the table. It hardly seemed worthwhile to get back to work now. Well, after all, if he wrote even a page a day he would be done in a year or so, wouldn't he. Cam was fussing. It was a quarter to twelve. Diana would be back by one.

For a moment he almost considered changing Cam as an excuse not to work. That was desperation indeed. Doubtless Cam needed it, he always did, but Alan didn't want to set any dangerous precedents. He just didn't know (or want to know) Cam well enough for that sort of intimacy, he told himself. Lying. Deep down he felt that it was woman's work, even if the woman was Diana. Woman the caretaker, man the creator. Unfortunately it's hard for a man with cross-cultural knowledge to take a firm stand on roles. He usually got round the problem by pretending that he hadn't noticed Cam's condition. "Oh is he?" he'd say in surprise. He had ignored some pretty conspicuous reeking and leaking in the interests of looking academically absentminded, otherwordly, though he sometimes suspected he didn't fool his wife. Still, perhaps because she loved him, she hadn't yet called his bluff. Or was it because she loved Cam and really liked caring for him herself? On that thought he was almost tempted to do it.

What he would in fact do, he decided, absently patting Cam's head and loosening more homemade kitty litter, was put him into his snowsuit and take him out to see if the mail was in yet. On a Wednesday, with clear weather, the plane should be more or less on time. Maybe he'd meet Diana on the way home from Naomi's, or maybe she'd already be in the crowd of women and children that hung around gossiping and playing near the post office on mail days.

He dropped Cam gingerly into his snowsuit and zipped him up. The cat looked hopeful. Alan knew what she was thinking. It was public knowledge that to get outdoors like a real animal, dogs or no, was the ambition of Mukluk's life; her wistful face poking up under the picture-window drapes was familiar to passers by her owner's house. Now she was weighing whether this tall, slow-looking human would be dumb enough to let her slip by him and out the door. Alan didn't intend to be that dumb. He wasn't even dumb enough to leave his dissertation work out so that Diana could see how little he'd done. He scooped it up and put it away just before he wrapped a muffler over Cam's nose.

Clutching the baby to his left (or outer) side, and fending off the cat with his right (or inner) calf, he squeezed through the door sideways and shut it behind him. Cam adjusted on his hip, Alan discovered that he had forgotten his own mittens. So much for a long outing. With one hand in his pocket and the other trickily arranged so that most of it came between Cam's body and his own, he began to hike along towards the center of town. Wino Day, lake and land, sparkled in the sun. As he neared the post office he could see that the plane had already come in, probably rather early, for the mail was sorted and being handed out. Now he could distinguish Diana, who saw him and waved a handful of mail. Something bulky – Eaton's catalogue must have come. He trotted a little faster, drawn by her orbital pull, which he could always feel as far away as he could see her.

He brushed his lips against her cheek briefly. One didn't do much outdoor kissing in this kind of climate. "Have a nice time?" he asked. He meant "You must have had a better time than I did. Have you missed me? I'm alive again now that you're back. What's Naomi got anyhow? Dammit, you have a look of accomplishment that I know *I'm* not wearing."

"Wild," Diana said. "Wait'll I tell you. Get a lot done?" But blessedly she didn't pause for an answer. Alan half listened as she chattered to Cam, wondering how she managed to live so efficient a life. *She* got things done. Everything she touched turned to satisfaction.

Whereas he – nobody in town except the damned cat had spent so unproductive a morning as he, Alan thought, feeling grateful for even that companionship in failure.

But Mukluk, when they walked into the kitchen, was sitting on the table looking smug. Briefly, Alan had the impression that she'd been picking her teeth. Then he realized that the dark toothpick extruding so jauntily from the side of her mouth was a tail.

CHAPTER FOUR

"But see here," Alan was saying three hours later as he and Diana lingered at the table that still held their dirty dishes from lunch. He looked at Diana, wound up from the excitement of her recitation, and spoke kindly and patiently. "You're an anthropologist's wife," he pointed out. "You're not supposed to take these things so seriously. Cultures have their quirks, that's all. And it's probably just a story anyway. Maybe they just made it up to see what you'd say. Natives do that to outsiders sometimes; they think it's funny. Don't get so excited, okay?"

"In the first place," Diana told him, her grey eyes going almost clear, as they always did when she got intense, "you weren't *there* when she told me. You don't know how she said it and I can't seem to tell you so you understand." She made a fist and just managed not to beat on the oilcloth with it. "In the second place, whatever you may be, I'm not an outsider to Naomi and she's never played a trick on me. And she wouldn't."

Alan toyed with the bean and tuna fish residue on his

plate, drawing scallops around the edge with the tines of his fork. He wished that he could think of something more tribal and arcane to draw, something that would subtly reinforce his authority as a scholar. As for the beans and tuna, they had failed utterly to conjure up sunny luncheons in Italy. Alan half listened to his wife. He and she had covered the territory to which they were now coming at least four times already, with minor differences in phrasing.

"It was Naomi's own grandmother who told it to her," Diana insisted. "It really happened at Mistassini Lake." Alan grated his teeth gently. The repetition of the name Mistassini annoyed him. It had begun to sound like the name of a person. Miss Tassini. Miss Tassini Lake. Mister Seeny. Mister C. Knee. Silly damned word. Next she'd talk about the priest.

"That priest put it in a book. Look it up if you don't believe her." Diana's voice rose. "It's exciting, god dammit, and moving and spooky. I *hate* it when you won't get interested and believe things. When Cam's old enough to listen I'll never tell you anything again. Can't you feel what it would be like for that child to hide outside the tent and know her dad and uncle were strangling her mother? I could see it when Sarazine told how they had those two strips of rawhide out either side so they didn't have to watch what they were doing when they pulled. And then that long time to burn the body. And that little girl saying it was the smoke that made her eyes water, because she thought she wasn't supposed to love her mother any more. God, Alan, I've never heard anything like it!"

Alan sighed. The facts didn't bother him. Despite what he'd said to Diana, it had probably happened, all right. He vaguely remembered cases of windigo psychosis documented in the nineteenth century and earlier, though he didn't recall any details. He had a general notion that family members were responsible for killing people who threatened to turn into cannibals. Further, he understood (if he didn't much like) how moved Diana was at Naomi's sharing the family scandal with her. You didn't tell family things to outsiders; when you did, they stopped being the outsiders they were meant to be. Or he supposed they did. He'd never tried it, except with Diana. Her accepting someone else's intimate tales (and telling? what was she telling?) seemed a kind of infidelity. Men couldn't, didn't, do that with other men. Why did women persist in it? Not fair. Not loving. Not *his*. What's more, Diana was always far too ready to embrace things outside the ordinary; she had an openness and receptivity that delighted him as it applied to himself, but that otherwise made him ill at ease. "Well, it could be true; how do you know it's not?" How many times had Diana hit him with that in the course of their relationship? The latest repetition had occurred not ten minutes ago. And she didn't mean it might be true that Naomi's great-grandmother had been dutifully executed by her male relatives. She meant that maybe the woman really had been turning into a windigo, that icy-boned cannibal that haunts the mythology of the northern Indians. He wondered briefly whether he should have brought Diana north at all, if bringing her involved exposure to a whole new body of superstition and folly.

Even their first meeting, in a ramshackle house in Florence, Massachusetts, the squarish sort of old house which on back streets is given over to student apartments, had been fraught with credulity.

This was before Toronto, when he was an undergraduate at U. Mass. He had come east to college, choosing U. Mass for no very specific reason, feeling a cautious desire to escape from the midwest into easternness without getting out of his social depth in anything too Ivy League. Life had been pleasant enough – if not rosy, a comfortable beigey pink. Most of his classes held his interest. He played a little tennis. He had some drinking buddies. His sot of a father, he remembered cheerfully every Saturday night, drinking night, was more than five hundred miles away.

In the spring semester of his third year at college there had moved onto his floor a raving eccentric with the mis-leadingly wholesome name of Chip, a boy with perpetually blackened eyes who believed that with the proper mind set he could rearrange his molecules and pass through closed doors. It had been fun to watch him try, and when Alan discovered that Chip was one of a group of amateur para-psychologists who met every other week in Florence, he got himself invited. He had some idea of using the things he saw to spice up a seminar paper on domestic conjuring and modern middle-class magic.

He had been the last to arrive that night, picking his way through two shadowy rooms and past the host's sleep-ing infant to find the assembled group. Of his host and hostess he afterwards remembered nothing except that one of them claimed to possess an aunt who could read the Bible through a layer of cardboard. There were per-haps a dozen guests, with most of whom he became familiar as the evening passed. A carpenter called Chan, who sat cross-legged on a white pillow, seemed to be in charge. A large, gentle-looking young man with a record of juvenile crime had arrived on a bicycle; he spoke from time to time of joining a monastery. Two adolescent chil-ren of Smith professors were there, swollen with pro-visional adulthood. Chip was on hand, of course, and moved over to make room when Alan came in. And there were at least three intense co-eds, of which he had noticed only one, and no woman ever again. Diana.

She was sitting against the wall, on the far corner of the studio couch, with her feet pulled up, wearing blue jeans and a silky, cherry-colored shirt. It was May, and when he looked at her he seemed to smell, for the first time, the lilacs outside the open window beside her. Sometimes when he remembered that night he could almost smell them still and see the headlights pass on the dusky street. The other girls had at once become lumpish and unkempt and humdrum. He forgot to make his slightly contemptuous notes about the goings-on and watched with the absorption of a convert while this woman someone had called Diana closed her grey eyes and identified with moderate success the colors of the kitchen sponges that Chan held behind his back, singly or in pairs. He savored the shape of her fingers and of her slightly out-thrust breasts, the hint of a nipple, as she in turn concealed the sponges for a philosopher's child. His sensations, unswervingly classic as they were, took him with all the violence of a disease in virgin territory.

By the time, hours later, that Diana lay on the couch to be hypnotized, all too receptive a subject, his heart was by a real-life mix of metaphors both on his sleeve and in his throat, and it was all he could do not to fling himself down on top of her and order the others out of the room. The sight of her artless but unnatural sleep called up protective, possessive responses new to him both in kind and in degree of sharpness. A happy ending and four years of marriage had failed to dull them.

When, feeling more than usually clumsy, he had asked to drive her home, she had acceded to his request with a mild surprise; she had been too intent upon the proceedings to notice him much before. On the way back in his car, while Alan wondered if DWI included intoxication by love, they had argued. "Maybe she *can* read through cardboard," he remembered Diana insisting. "It's called Eyeless Sight – why shouldn't it be true?" He had come to think of that line as Diana's motto and stigma: why shouldn't it, anything, be true? For her the world was dense with possibility, both magical and horrific, a viewpoint that he in his constricted universe deplored.

Her receptivity was not to be mistaken for weakness, he

had rapidly discovered. She was a lady made of steel and crystal inside – a good receiver, a good transmitter, but not what you might call pliable. It had taken him some time and mental agony to get her to bed, and much more time even to shake hands with the Diana inside. He was still awed that their union came voluntarily from such otherness, breathless sometimes with anxiety lest it be cut off, and always ravenous for more.

All these thoughts were so intact, so familiar, that they passed through his mind all of a piece, scarcely making a pause in the argument. "Right," he said, trying sarcasm. "Tell me about it. Old ladies certainly do that, change into windigos all the time. Skeletons and hearts turn right into ice. You have to kill them before they begin to eat the neighbors. Either that or put them into nursing homes down south where the neighbors are all too tough to get down. Hang onto your culture, can't you? At least it's ethnic for Naomi to talk about windigos; it's loony for you."

Diana was looking dogged. His heart twisted a little but his desire to put her right overrode his compassion. "She wasn't an old lady," she said, beginning to talk with her teeth closed. "She had a little girl, remember? Stick to the point. The woman herself believed that she was turning cannibal. The little girl heard her say that she was hungry for human meat. She knew why her mother had to be killed. You can't just pass off a family murder, a *reluctant* family murder, as some kind of mass delusion without even considering what really went on. Maybe she *would* have eaten somebody if she felt that way. How do you know if it's craziness or possession or if there's any difference? Hell, I wish I'd never brought it up, I really do. You're the only person I could tell, and you're no good."

She shrugged up from the table and scratched a new hole in the frost on the kitchen door. He knew that she was close to frustrated tears. The worst of Wino Day, in a way, was that the affectation of nonchalance was nearly impossible. You couldn't even pretend to catch a glimpse of something fascinating outside when you had to claw at the ice before you could see at all. It certainly complicated marital posing in moments of stress.

He pulled out of his pocket a letter from his mother that had come in the morning's mail. He had lucked out this time, having something real to do. This was probably the only thing a letter from his mother had ever done for him. He tore open the flap, noting with mild distaste the clump of daisies printed on the envelope. "Dear Son Alan," he read.

> Got a letter in the mail Tuesday and thought sure it would be from you but it wasn't. You and your family must have a lot to do up there and be too busy to think about the old folks at home, ha ha, though I don't know what you do up there without a TV even. I suppose you must have a lot of snow. I don't know how I'd get along without my TV here, of course I don't watch the daytime serials, I have enough troubles of my own – you know what I mean – but I do love my game shows. Well you don't want to listen to an old lady so I will just ask you how you're doing up there. I suppose it is very cold and you have a lot of snow. We are getting nippy here now but not what you would call cold I guess. We had a little snow last week but it didn't stick.
>
> Well I went to Chat 'n' Chew on Wednesday night and took some new bars with coconut and lemon. Everyone said they were real good and wanted the recipe. I know you don't like coconut but maybe you would like these and I will send the recipe to Diana if you write and

ask for it. Wish I knew her better. You and she are all I have if you don't count your father. And of course there's my big grandson I've only seen one time. How does he stand the cold? I hope you keep him wrapped up. My own boy a father, think of that!

Well it looks like it may storm here pretty soon. Is it stormy up there? I bet it's cold. Well no more for now from your loving

"Mother"

"Yes, god dammit, it *is* cold, 'Mother,' thank you," Alan said under his breath. His mother's letters always annoyed him, largely because they took longer to say nothing than the letters of any human he'd ever known. Then there was the matter of the signature. Why did she have to quote Mother as though it were a clever alias, a joke between them? Not that he hadn't had moments of thinking this pallid, ineffectual mate of his father's something of a joke at motherhood. He had contemplated the quotation marks long and hard. Now that he was a somewhat incredulous parent himself he wondered whether she'd found it impossible to come to terms with the label. Were the marks a way of protesting that she had a personal name, her own since infancy? No, he doubted that her thought process was that complicated.

Diana was still standing at the door, shivering a little now. How long could she look at the everlasting lake and a few black spruce? He decided to help her out. "'Mother' wants to know if it's cold," he offered.

"Tell her it is," she said through her teeth, wiping her cheeks with the back of her hand. But she turned aside to make more tea, still keeping her back to him. He understood her difficulty. Always before, in Massachusetts, in Toronto, she could fling on a jacket and go for a walk when his world felt too narrow for her. She'd come back looking more peaceful and he'd pour sherry when they could afford it and beer or coffee when they couldn't, and they'd be in balance again.

But here – where was there to go? A walk should look purposeful or else be an unqualified stroll. Walking along the lake on the skidoo tracks didn't seem like either one. Whenever he'd tried walking in moments of agitation he'd found that the gesture didn't come off anymore. He'd found, too, that outdoors he was inclined to nurse his wrath for the sheer physical warmth of it. Neither of them had perfected an exit, furthermore, that involved not only a jacket but socks and boots and hats and mislaid gloves. They were caged together as never before just when they seemed to need space. Perhaps there were a lot of reasons why they should never have come north.

CHAPTER FIVE

By late November their Christmas preparations were well in hand, as indeed they needed to be, for shopping was largely a matter of catalogue ordering in Wino Day. Though they had few friends or relatives to whom they might send gifts, Alan and Diana had relished the old-fashioned feeling of shopping from what their rural ancestors had so appropriately called a "wishing book." After only four months in the bush, they found the shiny riches of Eaton's catalogue overwhelming. For Alan the pages also called up a too-vivid picture of what Toronto looked like at Christmas, from the air, twinkling multi-colored out into the lake, and he suspected that Diana was harboring a similar memory, but they did not speak of it.

Instead they sat at the table with a blanket around their shoulders and chose some gifts for Cam – a red rubber ball and a plastic pulltoy like a fire truck ("We don't want him to grow up thinking that snowmobiles are the only vehicles," Alan said), and some new Dr. Seusses. A brown plush moose that was expensive but irresistible ("After all, he *is* living in Canada," Diana said). Three new pairs of sleepers, a size larger than the ones they'd come with, rosy (non-sexist), toast-colored (non-baby), and pale green (non-winter). They gave themselves up to be ravished by the photographs of Christmas cakes, recalling with nostalgia the magical back pages of their childhoods' catalogues, seasonal ranks of cakes and candies alluring beyond even the more pertinent pages of toys. Reminding one another of shocking airmail costs, they ordered a large round cake full of cherries and walnuts, frosted with almond paste and royal icing, embellished with paper holly. Caught up in festivity, they gave in to an extravagant box of four Christmas crackers gaudy with lace and glitter. "We'll give the extra one to Sarazine," Diana said. They added a dozen chenille candy canes and a paper frieze of Santa and his reindeer for Cam, and two strings of white lights, tiny so as not to strain the generator. For Naomi they chose a soft-looking red cardigan with pearl buttons, and a two-pound box of Laura Secord chocolate creams. Their gifts to each other were already hidden in separate bureau drawers.

An American cousin had arranged Alan's gift for his mother, Fruit of the Month for six months. It was a fairly expensive gift but not, he confessed to himself, very personal. Nor was this the first time he had given her such a gift. But then, he didn't feel very personal about his mother. She was a pale figure in his life, a little put-upon, a little inclined to whimper, no real protection against the explosion of his father. He knew that she had given him a steady, lukewarm affection, but the thought of her watching *The Dating Game* and eating the fruit of the month aroused no reciprocal feelings of warmth.

For his father, whom he still felt an ambivalent need to placate and attack, he had sent from Wino Day one of the region's most abominable tourist items, a beaver skin restuffed and trimmed with bead appendages. Diana insisted that it looked like a beehive hairdo wearing beaded oven mitts and slippers. Alan thought that certainly it looked more like a beaver lodge than a beaver. He hoped that his father would admire and think it expensive; he also hoped that the old man would open the package and think he had the DT's. From entirely different motives he had sent the smaller muskrat version to his supervisor in Toronto, who would be amused.

When they had first arrived in Wino Day, before the ground was altogether frozen, they had dug up and potted a scrubby little spruce tree from behind their rented trailer, telling themselves that they'd put it back next summer and that a winter in their back lean-to would be a treat for it. Cam was fond of the tree and gave it cookie crumbs when he got a chance. He would be pleased to see it decorated for Christmas, they thought.

The onset of deep winter also brought the caribou. Alan had been flattered to accept an invitation to a village hunt. He had relished in anticipation the sensation of speeding through the icy air to spread death on behalf of his household. Now he was discovering that in practice the icy air had its drawbacks. He was riding on the sled behind Willie Powderhorn's skidoo, trying to inch his face farther down into his parka to cut the sting. The Bay sold snowmobile masks, but everybody knew that one man's face had frozen to his mask the winter before, so they weren't very popular items. He and Willie had made a businesslike deal: Alan paid for the gas and helped with the work, for which he got his share of meat whether he shot anything himself or not. It was impossible, for the moment, to imagine that he would not. They had left before dawn, their sheer velocity bespoke aggression, their guns were in wonderful scabbards on both flanks of the machine.

After about an hour they stopped and built a little fire for tea-making while two skidoos that had started late caught up. None of the men said much. Alan squeezed his hands into his armpits, stamping his feet when nobody was watching him. The tea helped.

Later yet, about forty-five miles out from Wino Day, they saw eight dark shapes wandering on the frozen surface of the lake and made for them. Just as they cut their engines the herd began to run, but somebody in another skidoo had his gun ready and dropped the leader. After that it was easy. The caribou, demoralized, ran back and forth on the lake and died at every turn. The last caribou was only knocked down, not killed, and Alan suspected that might be his work (somebody else had fired at the same time), but when he started to creep up and finish killing it, Willie caught his elbow.

"Save bullets," he said, and jerked his head towards Baptiste, who was walking out onto the ice with an axe. With accustomed ease Baptiste made a long arm and cracked the animal on its head with the back of the axe. "Just as good," Willie explained, "and cheaper, hey? Come on; skin some, us."

Alan was puzzled at first when Willie, indicating a caribou, took axe in hand like Baptiste. Theirs looked dead enough, dead even beyond all amateur expectation. Then with revulsion he recognized Willie's intentions. He stepped back involuntarily as the cutting edge of the axe came down on the animal's neck. Willie chopped off the head with aplomb and maybe just a hint of a grin in Alan's direction. There was very little blood. Later Alan realized that the cold accounted for it. Liquid froze almost at once. Next Willie severed three of the legs at the knees, with one stroke each. He handed the axe to Alan with mock courtesy. "Last one for you," he said. Alan gulped, shut his eyes, and swung. The job was reasonably effective, if not very neat, but the feeling of cutting through bone! Not at all, really, like wood. Willie approved.

Together they pulled off the hide, which came away easily. That was better. Willie drew his knife a little way down the beast's belly, starting at the top, laying open the chest cavity. He handed the knife to Alan. "You do that one," he said. "Just open him nice, deep enough, not too deep or you won't like what happens."

Deep enough but not too deep – there were great instructions. Alan felt his tongue go between his teeth as he tried for the right unspecified depth on pain of who knew what. Then he saw what. Some loathsome, grey-blue, bulbous creature was swelling its way up through the slit. It looked like the back of a giant slug, a monstrous spider. It got bigger and bigger without revealing any further features while Alan tried to gather his wits and assess Willie's delight at his face. By the time the thing was the size of a beach ball, Alan began to suspect that it was some kind of internal organ, and glancing around he saw that the phenomenon was not unique to his own caribou. Tentatively he reached towards the object with the point of his knife.

"No!" Willie exclaimed, no longer laughing. "Don't prick! Stomach blows up. Makes awful mess." Alan stopped just in time. He'd had more than mess enough, and it was a gingerly man who helped Willie scoop the guts out onto the snow, saving the heart and kidneys.

The work was going well. At length the men grew conversational, almost open, over the plundered bodies and heaps of debris. Alan paid little attention at first. For one thing, he didn't understand much Chipewayan, and as every foreign-film goer knows, a conversation in which one understands only the conjunctions and none of the verbs is not very exciting. For another, he had retreated inside his head to imagine himself looking back on this satisfyingly picturesque business later, when he was some place warmer and tidier. But some current of tension in the conversation made him look up to see Baptiste standing in his bloody boots and saying something at which the other men nodded wisely.

Alan looked inquiringly at Willie, who was the closest

thing he had to a friend. They'd shared tea and bannocks at Willie's house, coffee and gingersnaps at his. Sometimes they and their wives sat together at the school movies.

"They say the village feels not so good anymore," Willie explained. "When they cut wood or carry water they think something hungry watches them. I feel it too, me. We feel it but we see nothing." He shrugged and tried to look casual, in case Alan should laugh. "Not much fun, eh?" he added. But Alan was suffused with joy at the utter anthropological rightness of such talk in the midst of this violent, red and white, masculine landscape. He looked at the skidoo-suited hunters with appreciative love, as though they were a lithograph miraculously put in motion for his pleasure. And there he himself was, part of the design, off to the lower right like a portrait of the artist.

The men, who were watching him too, began to talk among themselves in their own language again. Willie listened. "They want to know" he translated, "whether the – er, ah – whether you feel this." He had avoided some rude term, Alan perceived.

"I don't think so," Alan said, "not exactly." Damn. He had wanted only to observe. He smiled tentatively, not wishing to be blotted out of the picture, but he was uneasy. He did in fact recall the sensation of being overseen at his outdoor chores. He had always assumed, however, that Diana and Cam were watching him from the window, and, affecting to ignore them, he had nailed or shoveled or chopped with the extra flourish of a man onstage to an admiring audience. It crossed his mind briefly that he would not like to have been showing off for a hostile and possibly carnivorous arctic spirit of some sort, a notion which further conjured Proxene's weird fang-bearers. That annoyed him. "No," he said more firmly. Solidarity be damned, he didn't believe in spirits and he wasn't going to let his century down.

The men shrugged and went back to pulling viscera out onto the snow with their ungloved hands. They had not perhaps expected him to feel anything. "It only happens sometimes in the winter," Willie said a little apologetically, sweeping the horizon with his hunting knife. "Not in summer."

The trip back lacked the zest of the trip out. It was slower; it was darker; it was quite astoundingly cold. They had found no more caribou that day. The brief illusion of solidarity with the villagers had been broken by the conversation about spirits, though, to be sure, the men retained their unfailing politeness towards the stranger who was merely insensitive and perhaps meant well enough.

The thought of the animals that, while alive, had been a challenge to his prowess, to man against the environment, to all the clichés of the hunter buried under layers of urban living, now sent a bad taste all through Alan's head. He was hunkering in front of two of them, sometimes squatting on them reluctantly when his legs ached too much, sometimes standing on the sled runners from which he tended to fall off into the snow. The very idea of those huge chunks of freezing flesh, tagging and nudging behind, turned his stomach. They seemed a horribly tangible spirit of the animals that he had, in some sense, meant only to play hunter with. It was one thing to shoot them and see them fall down, quite another to bash them on the heads with axes so they couldn't get up and go away again when the game was over. As for the meat – well, really he didn't enjoy quite so visceral a connection between the killing and the eating; he preferred his meat to come on little styrofoam or cardboard trays with cellophane over it.

He was exhausted as well as cold, and was aching with muscle strain in both accustomed and unaccustomed places. He would have liked, surpassing even a week's vacation in the Bahamas, just to take a hot shower and ask Diana to pour him a double scotch while he lay down in their old Toronto apartment to watch television; he would joyfully settle, if he ever got home, for a hot wash-up of any sort and a scotch poured short to preserve their dwindling bottle, and a chance to lie down and just listen to his wife moving around the kitchen, maybe inveigling her to bed when he felt a little rested. The snow had almost stopped hurting his face, a bad sign, but by scrooching his cheeks around down inside his muffler and collar he produced an encouraging pain.

Four hours of iciness mixed with smells of blood and snowmobile exhaust brought him home, where bolstered by Willie's offer to stop by in a day or two and help him strip meat for drying, he heaved his portion of frozen flesh onto the roof of his lean-to, away from passing sled dogs, with a shiver of fatigue and nausea. And after the stripping, the lean-to would have sheets of flesh swathed on lines like raw, red lingerie. Now there was something to look forward to.

He was glad his father couldn't see the shiver. He couldn't bring himself to repeat even now the things his father had called him from time to time. There was the time he was six and had come home from fishing barefoot with his fish in his sneaker because he didn't want to touch it with his hand. There was the weekly struggle of wills over his repugnance to carrying out the garbage. Life with Diana was easier, was beautiful, and now she was only on the other side of the door.

Diana, however, when he kicked the snow off his boots and came into the warmth of the kitchen, hardly looked up at him. Though not unprecedented, this behavior was unusual. Alan privately considered it ill-timed, but decided to jolly it away.

"Here's the mighty hunter home from the arctic wastes," he ventured. Nothing. A wan smile. "Frozen, thirsty, starved for love," he suggested.

Sounds of infant cursing broke out from the cubicle off the bedroom, where Cam lay unwillingly in his crib. For once it sounded like a sympathetic comment on Alan's own state. He had it on good authority and some experience that nobody grows up on the inside, but several years had passed since he had felt quite so much like putting his thumb in his mouth and wrapping up in the nearest blanket. Backing nearer the stove, a gesture more atavistic than useful, he began to be aware of his toes again. They hurt. He pulled off his mittens stiffly, grateful that he'd worn two pairs, resisted the temptation of his thumb, which was still nasty with caribou anyway, and steeled himself to take Diana seriously.

Simultaneously she stood up and made an effort to look glad at his homecoming. "I'll make you a drink to thaw you out," she said. "Naomi's sick."

Alan felt a flash of rage that warmed him nicely. Hooray for anger. Who came first with Diana anyway, he prodded himself, him or some old Indian woman?

"Oh Alan," she went on in a rush, "I'm really worried. Sarazine says she hasn't eaten anything for two days and she won't talk. She just sits on the bed and won't look at them except when she thinks they don't see her. She didn't even act like she knew I was there, or else she didn't care. Her eyes look all empty and far away."

"Why don't they ask the nurse to look at her?" Alan said, impatient. He was looking at Diana and thinking, suddenly, that he wanted all of her, not just her ass or her legal allegiance or even that mythic organ poets identify with the heart, but every finger-tipping, eye-lashed, down-haired mote of her body and all her intangible self as well.

He wanted her inside, him inside, everyone else – Cam,

Naomi, everyone they knew or ever would know – on the other side of a great psychic chasm. The fierceness of his desire caught him off guard so that he choked and coughed.

"They already did," she said. "Drink this – you might as well finish the bottle – and you'd better take an aspirin," she added, handing him a munificent inch and a half of whiskey in a jelly glass. "The nurse said it looked to her like a clinical depression. What good is that? Nobody'll fly her out to the hospital for depression; half the town's depressed and crazy all winter. Besides that, she's old and she doesn't matter enough to anybody but me. Birthday parties are one thing and not giving up on her's another. She'll starve to death at this rate. Do you think I could make custard out of powdered milk?"

Remembering food then, she scooped a bowl of split pea soup from the pan on the back of the stove and put it on the table. She cut two thick slices of brown, homemade bread to go with it. Because Diana was doing it right, knowing that hunters on their homecoming require warm and comforting food (though she hadn't asked about their luck, had she), Alan ate despite his lack of appetite. As he ate, he thawed out and felt better, and Diana told him in (he felt) repetitious detail about Naomi's eccentric withdrawal and dangerous abstinence. He told her, in re-taliation, about the hunt – the number of caribou and who had made a good shot and how much meat he'd brought home. He did not tell her that the men of the village felt watched by something hungry, nor did he admit his own distaste for the afternoon's work.

When the plates were cleared, they went to bed early by mutual consent and made three-quarters of an hour's moderately satisfactory love. Alan fell asleep on a wave of warmth and mild contentment, but that night he dreamed again. Proxene's grinning, ice-slicked horrors went on leading their inscrutable lives beneath his skates, secure behind glass, where no broom could move them. Not even the axe helped much.

For ten days now Naomi had remained in her peculiar
state of withdrawal, silent, huddled on her bed, drinking
little, eating nothing, indeed looking frightened at any
talk of food and putting her withered finger to her lips.
Her decline had been steady, though less pronounced
than one would have expected. There was no recognition
in her inward-looking eyes of Elizabeth or Sarazine or her
wrinkled old husband when they tried to give her cups of
tea or bent over to care for her. Once or twice there had
been a flicker of something indefinable when Diana,
whom she had most recently loved, came in with useless
dishes of bouillon or crème caramel, but whatever it was, it
was less than a greeting or an acknowledgement.

On the tenth day Diana begged Alan to go with her. He
was doubtful, knowing himself an outsider and disliking
very much the prospect of whatever nastiness that low-
slung little cabin of Naomi's held for him. Moreover, he
sensed that Diana wanted him to "do something" about
the situation. He had felt unspoken pressure for several

days as she would report each visit's gloom and look at him expectantly. He had tried to pretend that she expected merely sympathy or interest, but he knew better. Surely there was nothing to be done. There was a nurse in town. The woman had family. And as for what Diana saw emerging as a rather odd familial attitude towards the old woman, some mixture of solicitude and distancing, his role as an anthropologist was to observe native behavior, not tamper with it. Neither he nor Diana having been raised within the tradition of any church, they both thought of a missionary's principal business as being the dissemination of literacy, sanitation, and frontal sex. There had been many a heated discussion in which Alan had asserted that his task was quite otherwise, while Diana asserted that in case of inhumane or cruel practices an anthropologist should espouse reform. When they had last had that argument, in graduate school days, it had been altogether theoretical ("Suppose you actually *found* a baby on an ice floe – "), but Alan could feel it coming on again in a practical context.

"But what can I *do*?" he asked now, hoping Diana had no answer.

"I don't know," she admitted, "but you can't do anything if you don't go. You could try to think of something. You're supposed to be a social *scientist*, aren't you?"

In the end he agreed to visit Naomi. They decided to take Cam along rather than leaving him with a neighbor on the way, for perhaps – Diana's idea – the sight of such a rosy, agreeable child would revive Naomi's interest in life. The walk to Naomi's was only fifteen minutes at a brisk trot; one did not linger. Cam clearly preferred to be carried by Diana, but Alan's long arms could better wrestle the round, heavy, slippery, and unwieldy bundle of Cam in his snowsuit, so they passed him back and forth like runners in a relay, trying not to break stride as the wind cut off their breaths and the packed snow creaked underfoot.

Too soon they found themselves outside Naomi's dark little house, facing the blankness of her weathered plywood door. Her granddaughter Sarazine answered their knock with a look that told them Naomi's condition was unchanged. Stooping a little, Alan went for the first time into the house where Diana had found a second home. Entering it as an anthropologist, he would have found it merely satisfying; aware of his obligatory social role, he found it all at once unnervingly foreign. Too small for his tall body. Too dark for eyes that had just come inside. Too smoky. Too crowded. There came to him suddenly that childhood perception, lost in the process of growing, that everyone else's house smells unfamiliar and slightly sinister. Diana moved there easily, and he felt doubly cast out.

He stayed near the door and peered around the room, surreptitiously sniffing, sorting the odors of smoke, sweat, boiling meat, greasy hides; they weren't unpleasant, just solid. As his pupils adjusted to the dimness, he perceived something bizarre about the walls. They were lumpy, irregular, not like walls at all. He began to see that they were festooned with useful objects – overcoats and cooking pots, pairs of snowshoes and work moccasins, tools. Boxes and shelves were nailed up to hold supplies. Alan thought he could see Diana's wooden jewelry box across the room; those must be Naomi's beading supplies. The domestic arrangements showed an orderliness that Alan admired even while he struggled with the feeling of being in an alien world.

The skins made it worse. Walls ought not be furry, they really oughtn't. There were horrid hairy bags hanging all around, beaver bags, looking as though they had nightmares folded inside: here comes the old sandman with his bagful of Ratfat dreams. They reminded him, too, of an illustration that had terrified him in childhood – a fox in high boots and a plumed hat, holding a great sack stuffed with a child it intended to eat. He had never let his mother open to that page if he could see it coming. It must have been the fox skins drying on the wall, in combination with the bags, that triggered that memory, he thought. The skins were dried inside out over forms, flattened and impaled like foxes possessed by the spirits of ironing boards. They were colored the greasy tan of old oilcloth; tufts of fur stuck out between their legs. Other skins, finished, hung fur side out again, nailed through their nose holes.

He looked around for the security of his family and saw Diana beginning to undress Cam for what he personally hoped was going to be a very brief stay. "Let me do that," he murmured, desperate to be busy. "You'll want to go see Naomi."

Slowly he finished unzipping Cam's snowsuit, peeling it down with one hand while with the other he clasped his son chest-high like a shield. Setting him back on a chair, he buried his face in the boy's neck for the familiar baby smell of him. Cam giggled in surprise at the tickle of Alan's moustache. Alan was glad Cam hadn't the words to comment on the unexpectedness of his parental attentions. He got the snowsuit stuck on the boots, and the boots stuck on the shoes, and the shoes stuck in the boots, all delays which rejoiced his heart. Looking neither to right nor to left, he untied the shoes and fitted them back on Cam's apparently boneless feet, first hitching up the socks. Cam watched dispassionately as Alan loitered, fumbled, and nuzzled. He was not deceived. At last, knowing he'd used up his delays, Alan lifted Cam down to play with Elizabeth's youngest, who was behind the door stacking a set of plastic blocks from the Bay.

Taking a deep breath and regretting it, Alan smiled sociably around at Naomi's family, who, straight-faced, were dealing a new game of three-handed cards at the table.

Last and reluctantly he took in the scene against the far wall where Naomi huddled on the corner of the sleeping platform.

Diana was kneeling on the floor, her back to Alan, parka cast down beside her, holding one of Naomi's hands in hers. The family, he thought, looked a little embarrassed at the emotional extravagance of her gesture, but they said nothing, politely examining their cards. He thought that he heard one of them say "Deal," but then he realized that they wouldn't be speaking in English, and that the cards were already dealt. He was far, very far, from his own context, but this place was home to them, with its familiar oil-drum woodstove, the Bay calendars layered on the door, the old illustrated-paper chromo of Queen Victoria that Diana had described as Naomi's pride, the inevitable Proxene production. Naomi's family were not perhaps happy, but they were calm.

This was Naomi and her husband's own house, tiny and, by her children's and grandchildren's standards, lacking modern refinements. Until Naomi's illness it had, again according to Diana, been preternaturally neat. It was not abominable now, but none of Naomi's family was the housekeeper she was. There were crumbs here and there, a little soot, a spill, a small pile of soiled clothing in the corner. Alan forced his unwilling feet to carry him across the floor to Diana's side. He could think of nothing to say as he looked down at the old woman.

She seemed to have shrunk since he had seen her last, a healthy worker of beads and leather and a teller of unnerving tales. She looked now like something from an unnerving tale herself. She was a mummy, a monkey-woman, a withered sibyl caged in her own bones. The claw that Diana had not enclosed gripped a bit of the blanket with the impersonality of pliers, and her flat dark eyes were inscrutable. Impossible to tell whether they looked at Diana with an unrecognizable degree of intensity, looked far away into another time and place, or looked nowhere at all. Impossible to tell whether anyone, and if anyone, who, was at home behind them. Her mouth, which he had somehow expected to find gaping, was clamped shut, the rigidity of her jaw proclaiming no more tea, no speech, no food, no food, no food. There was about her whole person a silent rigor as if somewhere she held back the enemy. Alan found that he himself had tensed and was beginning to sweat. He turned away and sank into a chair by the table, realized that he hadn't been asked, began to stand again, and was waved back into place by the old man, Naomi's husband, whom before he had scarcely noticed.

The old man was small like Naomi, a little thicker, infinitely sad of eye and resigned of mouth. "He knows she's dying," Alan said to himself. He tried for a moment to imagine how he would feel years from now if Diana were to predecease him, but his mind drew back from the pain as his hand would draw back from the stove behind him, and he gave it up at once. The look he shot the old man was so full of commiseration that for a moment he sensed a kind of reciprocal opening up. Some minutes passed as they drank together in silence the cups of tea that one of the women brought to the table. Alan burned his tongue and felt grateful for a sore place he could understand. He heard the murmur of Diana's voice behind him, saying unintelligible things to Naomi. What nonsense could she be so steadily talking to that half-comatose old woman? He heard incongruous giggles from the corner where Cam and the other child played, needing no language.

Because he had failed so far to identify some elusive element in the old man's expression, he turned his attention back, to find a nearly silent but formidable struggle of wills taking place between Sarazine and her grandfather. From time to time old Mr. Benoani jerked his head in Alan's direction, from which the latter at last surmised that Sarazine was being conscripted to translate a message of which she disapproved. His sympathy was with Sarazine, for he felt increasingly certain that he did not want to hear anything in the least controversial.

At last the old man said something abrupt that seemed to bring Sarazine around, or else she succumbed to the force of a personality stronger than her own. "My grandfather," she began in a low, shamed voice, "wishes me to tell you that two times, once when he was a boy and once when he was a young man, in this very village, he has seen the windigo."

Alan groaned inwardly, wondering whether Sarazine's embarrassment arose from her grandfather's craziness or from the coincidence with Naomi's own family skeleton. He experienced a few moments of deep regret that he had not chosen to be a banker in Minneapolis.

Mr. Benoani said something more in Chipewayan. "It was not the giant windigo who is taller than trees in the stories," Sarazine amended in the stiff phrases of translation, "but that more terrible windigo who takes the spirit of a person like you or me" ("Not like me, guys," Alan said inside his head to distance his growing horror) "and turns their bones and hearts to ice and makes them to have unnatural hungers."

Alan glanced at Diana, but her attention seemed still to be with Naomi. Let them get their lunatic tales over before she turned around and heard them.

"My grandfather says that you will not believe the old things," she went on translating between interjections from what Alan now perceived as Mr. Benoani's hideous old tea-stained hole of a mouth, "but he has seen. When he was a boy the shaman turned windigo and was very powerful. He ate his own sons one winter before he could be killed. And many years later that man's daughter, who was with her mother's people that winter and so was saved, she killed her man when he came home from the hunt and smoked and dried the meat. She had no children yet and had not long been married, or she would have eaten them too. Her uncle killed her. It was the thing he had to do."

Why was this fool of an old man dragging up these stories, Alan asked himself. Could he possibly regard them as social pleasantries? Was he trying to distract himself from his own more present troubles? The question was resolved by Sarazine's next reluctant assertion: "He says that his wife is now turning windigo. He knows the signs."

While Alan sat stunned, he was treated to a recitation of the signs – withdrawal, silence, fear of eating, coldness of the extremities – symptoms of any number of mental or physical disturbances, he felt certain. "So what does he intend to do about it?" he asked, rousing himself to sarcasm, which was after all better than no response.

Sarazine's face was simple and full of trouble. Her voice rang out in a sudden silence. "He says that she must be killed before she becomes dangerous. He says that she has kept his bed warm for more than fifty years and that he cares for her, but now she is being taken by the windigo and it is time for her to die."

A quick glance at Diana and Naomi showed Alan that they had heard. Diana half rose up, her face white and incredulous, her body protectively in front of Naomi's, but not concealing the unsurprised look of acceptance on the old woman's face. Her husband must have said this before, been saying it for days, in her presence.

"For the love of God, Sarazine," Alan exploded, "you went out to high school for a year or so; you can't believe this crap!"

Her expression had become unreadable. "Of course we won't kill her," she said, speaking naturally again. "What do you think – she's my grandmother."

"But what about this windigo stuff," Alan pressed. "You don't believe that, do you?"

Sarazine shrugged, looking evasive and suddenly sullen.

She ran her nails over the edge of the table and picked at a splinter. "My grandfather knows a lot," she said finally. "He's old-fashioned, but he's seen things. If she's got a windigo sickness, maybe there's something we can do, eh?"

Alan got up from the table in disgust – "if she's got a windigo sickness" indeed! – and stalked over to Cam's corner, snatching him up with a yellow block still in his hand. Cam howled and kicked as Alan began to shove him back into his snowsuit. Seeing his own hand shake, Alan knew that he was frightened. He was also mad at everyone in sight, including himself for not being anthropologically cool. And Diana – she had hardly looked around at them. Who did she think she belonged to? "Come on, we're leaving," he snapped at her as he recovered Cam's boots from under the chair.

She picked up her parka and moved towards him in a daze, looking back over her shoulder at the unresponsive Naomi. He helped her into her sleeves and jerked her muffler into a knot around her neck before he turned to make the reparation of proper goodbyes. But when he had only begun to hem and haw there was a stirring in Naomi's corner and everyone turned to look.

The old woman cleared her throat and spoke for the first time in ten days. Disastrously.

"Help me," she said in Chipewayan. "I have hunger," she added in her careful English, "for the meat and bones of my dear pretty friend Diana."

CHAPTER SEVEN

"Oh shit," Diana said, sliding down to sit on the kitchen floor and covering her face. Tears leaked through her fingers and she wheezed between sobs. Alan still felt muddled. Fifteen minutes ago, having left Cam off to play at the babysitter's, he had settled down with a yellow pad and two Bic pens to revolve the beginning of a new paragraph. "Evidence suggests"? "It seems possible that"? "Incontrovertibly"? "Only a total fool would fail to acknowledge"? He had just been deciding to let the evidence speak for itself when Diana had banged in from the cold, short of breath and very much upset.

"Is it Naomi?" he asked carefully. "Did she die?" Even if she had, he thought, Diana's reaction was excessive. But he got up and went to kneel on the linoleum beside her. Judgments aside, a chance to succor the woman he adored, and to revel, however briefly, in being the strong half of the partnership, was a chance too good to pass up.

He would have liked to pull her weight against his torso and he could have managed it if she'd been kneeling too, but she was so firmly planted on her bottom that he tugged her towards him in vain. Therefore he moved up against her and took off her woolly hat to lay his cheek on top of her head. Her hair, crackling with static, clung to his skin. It was cool and smelled a little smoky, like Naomi's house. Pulling out a limp, grubby handkerchief, he mopped at the leaks (he couldn't get at her face), taking care with the lovely bones of her wrists and knuckles. Tears were sogging into the wristbands of her jacket. She turned her face to his shirtfront and blotted her cheeks against it. Alan began to be aware of a few wool-muffled phrases. At first he was too absorbed in sensation to pay attention, but finally some impression that Diana was gabbling about tea and ice penetrated his glow. He shifted his now painful knees, forcing himself to pay attention.

"Tell me again, honey," he said, reluctantly holding her a little way from his body. He never moved away from her nowadays, maybe never had, without a feeling like ripping flesh, and a wild mix of desires involving Siamese twins, total immersion, and angelic interpenetration.

"They'll kill her," Diana hiccupped, "if they haven't already." She struggled to control her breathing. "Sarazine and her mother and the old man, they're trying to m-melt the ice in her and make the windigo go away; they think, they say, she's all ice inside. She told them she wanted to eat Sarazine too. Let her! They're all just – just *meat* compared to her anyway. She's fed *them* – " Diana's voice rose and broke. "They've sucked at her until she's all dried up and now those pigs won't even – " Here her fresh assault on speech ran down and she wept on a high indignant pitch.

Alan shook her a little and wondered whether he could bring himself to slap her if she produced unmistakable hysterics. He'd hate it, unless of course he turned out to like it, which would be worse.

"Cut it out, now," he said, an edge of anxiety in his voice. Diana tried. "What are they doing to melt it?" he asked, awful visions of slow roasting, of gasoline and smotherings under blankets and penetration by hot pokers harassing his imagination.

"They're giving her hot tea," Diana said faintly. Alan almost giggled in the giddiness of his relief.

"Through a funnel," she added. "You have to stop them."

Alan still hoped, as they trotted to Naomi's and he struggled to fasten his parka on the way, slowing only a little to accommodate the painful stitching of Diana's side, that Diana had over-reacted. If only he could run to the rescue and find no rescue necessary, if only he would find a scene of plausible home doctoring, a feeding tube suggested by the nurses and eccentrically misinterpreted by Naomi's family. But he hoped without much strength of conviction, for it had been gradually dawning on him that he had come by accident to a place in the world where life and death took themselves seriously. Sometimes all his past life seemed a kind of illusion. And the illusion, in its way, had been infinitely appealing, he now perceived. Even with his father there had been some degree of pretence and role playing, hostility that was partly ritual. Birth announcements in the old life pretended that babies were more like teddy bears than parasites; weeping brides and shotgunned grooms married with bells and confetti and orange blossoms; crones in nursing homes wore ribbons in their hair and corpses in coffins wore make-up. These lies seemed to him not silly but endearing, like sun lamps and grass rugs. But here life was close to the white bone, and contrary to the cliché, he did not find the meat there sweeter.

They were across from the schoolyard now, where children swarmed on the icy monkey bars and dropped on one another like cougars. He could make out their high voices singing, with great glee, something about a cowboy dressed in red. His spirits lifted a fraction of an inch in hopeful Unicefy warmth at the though of universal childhood, even at the thought of his own Cam, and he was a little tickled besides at the idea of Indians singing about cowboys. Then he began to catch the words –

> . . . fell off his saddle,
> Fractured his head.
> Blood on the saddle!
> Blood on the ground!
> *Great big blobs of blood all around!*

The tune, something like "Ninety-nine Bottles of Beer on the Wall," was compelling, and though he trotted fast enough to avoid the next stanza, which struck him as being worse and was certainly louder and even more full of gusto, the refrain of great big blobs of blood kept repeating itself ominously in his head.

There were not big blobs of blood all around at Naomi's, but that was all that could be said for the scene. Certainly there were people all around – Naomi's husband and two of her daughters and one of her sons; Sarazine, without her babies; Sarazine's sister Agnes with one of hers; and, dismayingly, Proxene Ratfat, who by some mysterious psychic tuning was always at hand for disaster or drama or rites of passage, emerging uninvited but not unexpected from her covered, patched, stuffed, insulated and generally be-nested packing box lair at the edge of the village. Only a few people could remember the unlikely origins of her hut, which now seemed a feature of the landscape.

Proxene's outfit this winter, and most winters, was a cast-off ski jacket over layers of sweaters, with a sprigged calico skirt hanging halfway down filthy polyester pants. But on momentous occasions like this one, Proxene was accustomed to top off her kerchief with a man's felt hat, trashed by some forgotten teacher or Bay employee in days of greater formality. Proxene, with the hat, was a bad sign; Alan hoped Diana wouldn't think of that.

But Diana seemed hardly to notice Proxene sitting in the corner of Naomi's kitchen, parka perpetually on, her stench covered by and absorbed in the oppressive smell of ammonia that rocked Alan at the door. As Naomi's daughter Elizabeth turned again to the stove with her dipper and two of the watchers stepped aside to confer, he could see Naomi on the ruined mattress and understand that tea was not after all a more innocuous remedy than roasting.

Blankets had been bound around her torso and tied, apparently with the dual intention of restraint and insulation. In any case, Naomi seemed too weak or resigned to struggle. They had propped her shoulders up a few inches, enough to let gravity assist the tea but not enough to put her mouth out of the horizontal. A piece of black rubber tubing – where they had found it and how they had got it down her did not bear contemplation – protruded just far enough above her lips to contain a metal funnel, into which her indefatigable daughter was pouring dippersful of tea.

It was as though the family, having found a thing to do, were compelled to keep on doing it until some natural conclusion. They looked as though they could go on dipping tea all night from the great vat simmering on the stove, aiming it at the now impersonal bullseye of the funnel mouth. Surely no human could ingest so much liquid and live, or tolerate so much heat. Naomi's body was expelling the liquid as fast as it could. Her clothing, the edges of the blanket, the mattress all around her were soaked with urine and sweat; sweat drenched her face and hair, assisted by tea; tea, spilled from the dipper, had scalded her face and neck, splashed her shoulders and the top of the blanket. Moisture oozed down the side of the platform and spotted the floor. Involuntary retchings made the tea in the funnel boil and spill back, Alan could see from his height as he tried not to retch in sympathy, but at last it seeped into her already bloated body and her tormenter turned for another dipperful.

Even Alan was forced to admit that whatever his duty as an anthropologist might be, his duty as a human being obliged him to do something about Naomi before they drowned her. But what, in God's name, could he do? No event or predisposition of his past life had in any way prepared him for heroism. Although he had often enough jeered in his heart at the behavior of his fellow men, he had never that he could remember stood out against a group of them straightforwardly. In all his make-up only his love for his wife burned with the fervor of purpose pertinent to heroism, and now he perceived that even that was flawed by his greed for more, and he was sad for himself. Fleetingly he understood that he had not wanted Naomi to live since her inopportune remark about eating Diana, not because he feared for Diana's life (the little old woman was clearly harmless) but because she had no right to harbor an idea so intimate nor to detonate it in his own head. But none of this told him what to do.

"Don't you think that's enough?" he asked feebly, stepping nearer the bed, but not too near. No response. He went closer. They barely glanced at him, but the glance said, "Stranger, back off." Alan backed, looking at his wet, retreating tracks instead of Diana's face. He imagined that he could see from the corner of his eyes her dawning contempt, a look that seemed to promise an infinite withdrawal. Panicking, cursing silently every creator of the universe known to comparative anthropology, he steeled himself to try again. Just then Naomi groaned and retched up the tube and funnel with a great fountaining of brackish water. Her body arched stiffly in the bed, and she fell back with a high wail and was still. Everyone, for his own reasons, looked abashed, except for Proxene Ratfat, who stood up for a better view.

The family retreated a bit (Elizabeth took the dipper and dropped it into the vat) and then re-formed around the bed as old Mr. Benoani walked up with his hunting knife. Alan, remembering the caribou hunt, opened his mouth in unaccomplished protest but shut it again when he saw that this was merely a tool to cut the cord binding the blanket. Several of Naomi's relatives bent over her corpse to do something that Alan couldn't see. Once the bodies parted and one of the daughters turned to drop the blanket behind her with a sodden thud, then bent back over the bed. The family spoke to one another softly. At last they drew away and Sarazine addressed the visitors. "My grandfather says her belly is hard," she reported, "and by that he knows her truly to have been windigo. The ice did not melt and nothing could be done."

Unwrapped, Naomi lay curled and wasted in her liquid bed like a dead shrimp in a tidal pool, and even Alan the secular man felt that some spirit, if not the windigo, had been expelled to bring about such a reduction. Diana beside him wept quietly with pity and emotional exhaustion. He would have liked to weep himself, for his own weakness and for human ignorance and even for Diana's lost mother figure, no longer competitive, the memory of whom now quite overwhelmed the carnivorous gnome of the last few days.

Proxene, who had snuffled over to the bed, was standing in silence, flapping her hat like a fan between herself and Naomi. It seemed a ceremonial gesture. The family conferred quietly at the table. What was supposed to happen now? Alan shifted from foot to foot, feeling superfluous, and thought of undertakers, death certificates, police, winter vaults and floral tributes, but none of them made any sense in Wino Day.

"What now?" he whispered to Sarazine, pulling her aside at the first chance. More than ever as he looked into her knowing eyes he suspected that the scene was unfinished.

She looked away. "Grandfather says we have to make sure the windigo is gone so she can rest quiet," she muttered.

Alan remembered Diana's account of body burning and pushed it violently away. "Well you can't get any more tea into her now," he said, feeling at once like an ass.

"They will have to drill a little hole in her chest," Sarazine explained reluctantly, "and pour it in."

Some tiny sound, perhaps, or sympathetic vibration, caused Alan to whirl around to his right and find Diana, who had been standing at his shoulder without his knowing it, toppling to the floor in a silent faint. He caught her and went down with her to break her fall, and as he knelt, for the second time that day, with Diana in his arms, he looked up to see Proxene Ratfat approaching him with a terrible fixity of interest on her round face, holding out a helpful cup of tea.

CHAPTER EIGHT

"Christmas is coming," Alan whistled dolefully into his muffler on his way to the Bay store, "the geese are getting fat, please to put a penny in the old man's hat." He broke off the words in his mind because they seemed to be getting away from him and meaning horrid northern things. Christmas was indeed coming the day after tomorrow and they indeed owned a dead goose, compliments of Willie. Theirs still had feet and a face, matters unfamiliar from Dickens but with which he would have to cope. As for the old man's hat, he knew that it should mean "the hat of the old man," but the words kept sticking together in the wrong pairs and suggesting Proxene's portentous head-gear, her old *man's hat,* which in turn suggested Proxene herself and brought his thoughts unwillingly back to Naomi, all too often the end of his mental trail.

Naomi was safe in her grave now, and Alan wasn't even sure which way he meant "safe" – that she was safe from the ill-conceived ministrations of her relatives, or that she would no longer trouble his marriage with either love or lunacy. Like many things in this inhospitable frozen place (conversation, affection, mobility) the old woman's hole in the earth had been hard come by, fought out of winter's grip with successive fires and scrabblings at the thawed earth. Flame and thaw and scrape, flame and thaw and scrape. That was how they buried Indians in the cold season. An unbidden image of Naomi curled under the rubble of half-frozen dirt (gone clear as ice to his vision) had struck him on the day of her burial and had recurred at least once a day ever since. He would look towards the lake and suddenly imagine her under the ice. Any clear surface, water in a basin, his shaving mirror, might seem to contain her form. Sometimes the picture came into his mind with no external prompting.

He was ready to get away from the house. The afternoon was near its end. He was restless. All day he had been in the house with Diana and Cam, and although he loved at least one of them, he felt now as though he had been let off a tether. Diana, who had been ill, was cranky. He had not once pleased her all day, as far as he knew. Everything he offered had been too late, too soon, too hot, too cold, too loud, too clumsy, too stupid, too *there*. Now he was working off his foiled solicitude and saving his mental equilibrium by an expedition to the Bay, where he hoped to find some lovely surprise.

Quite often a single unlikely species of food would appear with a new order – shrimp rolls, cheesecake, once (curiously) fish and chips. A good find might be his best move all day. He imagined coming home with something wonderful, something neither of them any longer remembered the existence of. He would laugh and hold the bag behind his back and say, "Guess what," and Diana, though she might still be cross at the first, would begin to be intrigued. Something friendly would come into her eyes and she'd say, "Well tell me, dammit" and maybe even grab at the bag. Then when he showed her how he'd brought home the better-than-bacon she'd soften and let him hug her. Then after they ate —

His happy fantasies had brought him nearly to the store. He could see through the lighted windows that it was doing a brisk business, or at least serving its unofficial mission as a gathering place. Three little boys were jumping on the long, broad front steps where their parents would lounge in good weather. He recognized the one in front as belonging to Willie's brother. Alan liked the very name of the place – the Hudson's Bay Company. Whenever he ceased to find privation picturesque, he would stifle his lust for electronic entertainment by sneaking off to look at the manly appurtenances sold in the back of the drygoods section. He would remember, as he gazed at the axes and paddles, his vision of the great white Jack London wild, and his chest would expand under his parka. Ranks of black rubber boots made his fingers twitch for a fishing line. He would walk home spitting imaginary tobacco juice and feeling nineteenth century and pioneerish.

He stamped over the doorsill and found himself in the midst of an amiable crowd. The store, an inevitable social center, had been wisely arranged with empty floor space by the entrance. Some people were shopping – drygoods on the left, groceries on the right. Drygoods was doing a better trade than usual, Christmas being so near. The others were gossiping and joking. Wiping the condensation from his moustache, Alan feigned a sociable punch or two in the right places. He admitted to the local nurse that Cam was wintering well. He asked after the health of the town cat. But his mind was out in front of him, foraging for Diana.

He knew that the drygoods section would be no use. She wanted no towels, tools, buckets, guns, or yards of flannel. Still less did she want Wino Day's taste in clocks or knick-knacks. There were very few beads and only a little embroidery floss. What she would perhaps like – Alan picked it up although it did not answer his original purpose – was a local favorite in Christmas decorating, of which the Bay had only one left. It was a kind of expansible festoon made of metallic paper, in an especially vivid blue that had caught Diana's eye at their babysitter's. There four festoons met in the middle of the living room and gave place to a long gold and red tassel of the same material. Wino Day seemed to decorate from the ceilings down more than from the surfaces up, he had noticed. Some reflection of the sky as the dominant feature of the landscape? Fingering the festoon's scalloped edges he strolled over to the shelves of food.

The selection, in eccentric ways, was better than one might have imagined. Cookies, for instance, poptarts, that sort of thing – they constituted perhaps one-fifth of the available groceries. He might in a pinch hunt for a kind of cookie they hadn't had, but he was hoping for something more striking. He would put off until last the frozen food bin where his prize might lurk. The canned goods were decent, though expensive. Maybe a can of ravioli sometime this week. They hadn't had that since last month. Had Willie not donated their goose, they might have tried to prop up a limp canned chicken and call it Christmas dinner. They had already bought the applesauce for the goose. He would assume that Diana was going to feel like coping with the question of vegetables tomorrow. The selection in the bins just now was rather good – turnips, carrots, celery. There was some sad lettuce, but no tomatoes or peppers this time, so salad was out. The bananas were frozen again and would be rotten under their uninviting skins. He could barely bring himself to look at the black lumps of always abominable meat.

He was getting nearer the refrigerated section where he hoped for surprises. He tried turning his back and counting rolls of paper towels. No use. The time had come.

Crossing his fingers in his pockets, he sidled up to the case and began to skim his eyes from right to left. Wasn't that blue and yellow package new? Anything good? Yes, by damn, it was waffles. It exceeded his expectations to find something so right for a wintery convalescent supper. He splurged on a package of frozen sausage and fetched some syrup from amongst the jams and jellies, feeling more holiday cheer by the moment.

Some unusually pleasant childhood memory of waffles drove him to the cocoa, though he'd not drunk any in years. He began to remember a yellow mug and white curtains with tufts. His grandmother's, then. And yes, there was his grandmother's voice saying "Of course it *isn't* about waffles" and reciting "Animal crackers, and cocoa to drink/That is the finest of suppers, I think." With an affectionate nod to his grandmother's memory he picked up three packages of animal crackers, glad that the Bay had them in stock. Time to start Cam on being a member of the family. He could almost see him at six or so, tall, dry articulate, reasonable. Lovable, even. Self-sufficient, not always pawing and sucking at his mother, not always in the way.

When, cheered, he paid for his selections and began to bundle up, he saw that even Proxene Ratfat was out socializing. A reason in itself, he thought unkindly as he arranged his muffler, to wrap up one's nose. Everyone gave her a word or two, nobody engaged her in conversation. She hung on the edges of the group, looking satisfied. Could Proxene's emergence mean that Santa Claus was due for a crash landing this year? Hoping to see a little reindeer blood, Proxene? he smirked. Rudolph with a doll carriage up his ass? You're a day too early. He tried not to notice that she was staring at him. For once he wished, not feared, that unzipped trousers might explain his fascination, but he didn't even bother to feel; you notice that sort of thing at forty below. There was something else. Never moving her eyes from his, she wiped her nose on the back of her hand and nodded.

It was almost night outside now. The Dantouzes alone of all the visible village had light bulbs on an outside tree. So it really was Christmas here too. He hugged his package. For an instant he remembered his parents' whole street gaudy with colored bulbs and window trim. The lights had made little splotches of color on the ice-crusted snow by the doors. Too much, he told himself. Excess. One tree was better because you appreciated it more. He'd take Cam out to see it.

Fifty yards down the street he turned back at the sound of bells and saw the best thing of all: a dog sled was whipping across the lake against the last glow of the horizon. Someone was coming home for Christmas after six or eight weeks of trapping. He could hear the dogs barking closer, and now the bells on the driver's short whip rang louder. His heart squeezed with love as the sled rose over the bank of the lake and swept into the town. There was Christmas indeed, with bells and joy and home-for-the-holidays and winter furs. As always, his first thought was of telling Diana. He wished she could have seen it. He turned home to find her, without whom no pleasure was complete. He was no part of the townspeople who had come out to greet the sledsman.

Still off balance with emotion, he thought once again of Naomi, who was also shut out, cut off from Christmas this year for the first time since her birth. Naomi's ostracism from the living was especially poignant, for she had been pushed out of life by the same people who had barricaded her in the earth. Alan found himself grieving for her a little. Having allowed so much in, he fished for the unidentified thought that still pricked at him. It was Proxene Ratfat – not the prospect of her unimaginable Christmas, but the fact that she had recognized him and nodded like an old friend.

CHAPTER NINE

By Christmas Day the presages of withdrawal that Alan had glimpsed in Diana's face when Naomi died were proving all too accurate. His response swung between simple disappointment about the day and a kind of numb despair, nearly bumping anger on one end of the arc and tears on the other. He had long (though perhaps not lately) anticipated the holiday as an occasion of intensified closeness with Diana, imagining the two of them snug and tipsy in front of the tree, one person almost, while fat, unlikely snowflakes fell outside and Cam, clutching his new plush moose, gave way to an uncharacteristic desire for early sleep. He should by now have been feeling warm-hearted and well fed, in love with his family, wise and male and benevolent in the northern wilds. Instead he felt hungry, perilously weepy, more than somewhat drunk, and as lonely as he could ever recall feeling.

He sat in the kitchen by himself, watching Diana and Cam through the open doorway to the bedroom, and tried to sort out what had gone wrong. Certainly things had been awry ever since Naomi's death. That night Diana had gone silently to bed after a perfunctory feeding of Cam, and though she had clung to him in her sleep and allowed him to care for her during the days of illness that followed – fever, exhaustion, weepiness, mild nausea, all of which might have been psychological since neither he nor Cam caught it – she had seemed to drift farther and farther away.

Naomi's body had been put away while Diana was ill. Neither he nor, so far as he knew, Diana had heard any more about the windigo business; neither of them, so far as he knew, had asked any questions; neither of them, he knew too well, had ever spoken of it to the other. Diana had perversely and without comment been wearing the red sweater which was to have been Naomi's Christmas gift. Alan admitted that it fit her and shouldn't go to waste, and supposed that in some way it made her feel closer to, maybe warmed by, her lost mother-figure, but it gave him the creeps. For one thing, he had never managed to shake Naomi's deathbed scene free from the schoolyard phantom of the blood-clothed cowboy: "dressed in red" sang in the back of his head about every third time he noticed the sweater. Besides that, it kept Naomi on his mind and the thought of Naomi made him feel guilty. He still didn't see quite how he could have saved her, for she must surely have been past recovery when he arrived at her house, but he had a nagging feeling of failure in some broader context of behavior.

Diana never accused him, though he sometimes thought he saw accusation in her eyes. But then, she seldom spoke to him at all, not really spoke. She was polite for the most part, as one is polite to an unwanted seatmate on a Greyhound bus. He wondered whether he was only imagining it, or whether she deliberately walked out of a room when he walked into it. He thought it was true, and the more he watched the more it seemed to be so. He fancied that she had begun to look annoyed, as though he were following her, when he came into any space she was occupying. For the last few days he had made a bumbling effort not to be in the same room, partly in hope of being conciliatory, partly lest he himself come to believe that he was begging at her heels. All that this had got him was a keen notion of how hard it is conspicuously not to follow somebody around a three-room trailer. He had begun to feel a little angry.

Her coolness to him had been counterpointed by an obsessive, crooning attachment to Cam, as though all her warmth was being blown down one pipe instead of two. She held and carried him more than usual, lingered over his feedings and changings and bathings, napped with him on the big bed instead of leaving him in his crib. Cam, naturally, was overjoyed, and the mother-child bond almost visibly thickened. Alan reminded himself over and over that this was not a proper cause of grievance against Cam, that he himself would revel in attention like that, was starved for it in fact; but trying to be fair and put himself in Cam's place led swiftly to cankering reflections on breasts and beds and the fact that he *should* be in Cam's place, that Cam was in his place, and so back to the grievance. The strain of looking as though he didn't care was making his face sore.

They'd both made some effort for Christmas, he and Diana, but they couldn't quite get in sync. As one advanced a little, the other would retreat in surprise (his) or fastidiousness (hers), and then they'd try again and fail again. The false starts were more productive of melancholy than the outright coldness. Visions of a long bleak life in which he and Diana never again managed to communicate stung his eyes.

Fearing to weep like an idiot at his own kitchen table, he gripped his drink – his fifth? fourth? sixth? – and turned his mind to the objective sequence of the day, hoping to find signs that Diana still loved him, or at least patterns that would suggest some useful strategy of reconciliation.

They had trimmed the tree, more or less in silence, the night before. "This side needs something more" cannot be construed even by the very hopeful as conversation. They had not especially meant to observe the tradition, never theirs before, of trimming on Christmas Eve; rather they had put it off from sheer inertia until Diana had suggested that they might as well wait a few days more and let Cam have the surprise of the tree on Christmas. Cam had been delighted – that part had been a success, though Alan knew in his heart that Cam's childish glee was something he could take or leave. There was his favorite tree, dressed up and shining and come in to visit, with packages underneath. He'd loved all his toys – slavered on his ball and slammed his fire truck into his father's shins and buttered the nose of his moose. The new sleepers hadn't interested him much, but he was wearing one now and looking fat and satisfied while Diana read to him.

Alan and Diana had exchanged their own gifts, so long hidden with expectations of loving unwrappings, with some embarrassment. He especially felt shy, as if his new stance of not much caring was debunked by his handing over tangible acknowledgements that he had cared very much indeed when he bought the gifts. The glossy art books were not so revealing, though only pretty fervent love would have smuggled anything so heavy in its suitcase. "Only flowers, candy and books, my dear" came back to him as the formula for decently impersonal gifts of courtship in an age of greater propriety. And here he was, dammit, courting.

The other gift he had almost held back, but he still cherished some hopes for it, and the books didn't seem enough. It was a bracelet of thick silver wire, a rigid circlet made to be worn either on the upper arm or more loosely around the wrist. He had commissioned it from an artisan he knew on Markham Street and had been delighted with the result. The silver strands played in and out and around one another until they met on the front in a kind of love-knot, holding a bit of polished garnet in their center. Some dreams came with it.

He and Diana had made little jokes about shackles when they were married, both eschewing wedding rings, and the jokes had been revived from time to time (though not lately) in tender and bawdy contexts. He'd had a happy, recurrent fantasy, since he'd bought the gift, of Diana wearing nothing but a silver slave bracelet, that bracelet, on her upper arm and kneeling in mock obeisance at his naked feet or dancing above him on the bed while the bracelet gleamed in the moonlight. More sentimentally, he had sometimes regretted not having put a ring on his woman's finger, some token more durable than flesh to signify their union, and he hoped that Diana would understand his need and wear, even want to wear, that bracelet around her wrist on a regular basis.

But after the nervous prickles at the back of the neck as he watched her fingers pulling red ribbon and silver paper off his silver and red offering, he didn't even know how to read her reaction. She had smiled perfunctorily and said, "Oh thanks, how pretty. Did you get it in Toronto? It will look super with my black silk shirt," and she hadn't put it on, not even to try it. That left Alan debating whether she had understood perfectly well but refused the ramifications of the gift, or whether they were so far out of communication that she didn't know the bracelet was supposed to say anything. He also wondered which was worse.

She had given him a bottle of very fine whiskey, which must have cost her some effort and energy to conceal. Against his will he had been a bit touched, but by now he had finished half the bottle in a fit of angry greed made worse by a reluctance to think about the future for which he should be saving some of it. Her other gift to him had been especially awkward for them both. A soft lumpy parcel in green and white striped paper, which he opened with apparent nonchalance, had held the most glorious pair of mukluks he had ever seen. They were soft caribou hide, decorated with two rows of martin fur and stiff with beading. They glittered in the light like someone's crown jewels, flower petals and leaves in sparkling reds and purples and greens, smooth under his hand. He had been awed into silence.

"I had Naomi make them for you," Diana had said, a little huskily, not quite looking at him. Alan perceived what it had meant to Diana to give them up to him after all that had happened. That was the moment, he thought later, when he should have swept her into his arms and met her gesture. Instead, abashed, he said "Oh" and kept looking down at them.

He sighed and dumped a little more scotch into his glass, not even bothering this time to water it. Then there had been dinner. Had he begun drinking then? He thought there had been a bottle of wine. His vision was beginning to go in and out of focus with his latest drink and he thought briefly about stopping. A growly inner voice he didn't remember detached itself from the rest of him and vetoed the idea. "Watsa matter," it jeered, "got to drive? Let 'er rip. Blotto. Plastered. Shitfaced. She'll be sorry."

Dinner. Dinner had been awful. Not just socially awful, though that too, but gastronomically awful. Willie's wild goose had seemed exactly the right thing, the perfect combination of traditional and arctic Christmas dinner. They had even taken the advice of their neighbors, sacrificing the visual to the culinary, cooking the goose in pieces with vegetables instead of roasting it whole, but it didn't taste at all like tame goose, and certainly not at all like Christmas. Alan thought that it tasted more like liver, curiously, than anything else. Perhaps it had been feeding on something peculiar. Neither of them ate much of the meat. The applesauce that went with it was fine but Cam got most of that, got most of everything nowadays. Their Christmas dinner was mostly bread and butter and goosey vegetables and mail-order Christmas cake.

Alan had been hungry all afternoon but had sulked and drunk instead of eating. Eating instead of suffering seemed in some unidentifiable way to be giving in. He nursed his resentment while Diana and Cam, who seemed not to share his misery, napped and cuddled and frolicked beyond his reach. Diana's voice in the bedroom droned soothingly on while he thought about dinner and wondered how she could be so warm to Cam, so cold to him. The bedroom lurched and reeled in the glow of Naomi's red sweater as vague images of emotional spigots and thermostats fuddled in his brain.

Only cold for him, he thought crossly, except his feet, which were warm, almost hot, but not because Diana cared now. He had put on his mukluks earlier, hoping to redeem his graceless "Oh." He had done it in a moment of love, knowing that he had been hurt by Diana's not wearing the bracelet and wishing to spare her a similar pain. If the gesture reached her, she gave no sign, but although the temperature of his feet had been rising steadily, he felt awkward about taking the mukluks off. At least he had not put on the requisite extra socks, though the caribou leather slapped around loosely without them. Slap, he thought, wagging his leg and peering at its end. Slop.

Dinners, food. Dickensian dinners with puddings like hot cannonballs. Perhaps they should have spent the year in London. Real geese for dinner there, god bless us every one. Mince pies. Boar's head carols. Wassail bowls. Punch, made with whiskey. He began to nod and came to with a start at the shock of seeing a roast suckling pig, apple in mouth, steaming on the threshold of his own bedroom.

But where was its platter? And why weren't its ears –
Further identification of the suckling pig brought him
several degrees nearer sobriety.

It was Cam, after all, Cam folded up on his stomach in
his rosy sleepers, new red rubber ball still against his slack
lips. The day had been too much, Alan said to himself,
when he saw his own little suckling pig as a suckling pig.
What he tried not to remember was the brief feeling of
hungry anticipation that the vision had provoked. Even
now Cam looked a little edible. Wise, perhaps, to go to
bed, only it was too early even though it was dark again,
and nowadays bed was only for sleeping.

While he hesitated, standing by the table, he thought
he heard shouts in the distance. He listened harder, skep-
tical about his senses. There were shouts, certainly, shouts
of angry or excited men in a pack. Feeling that providence
had come to his aid with an appropriate activity – was not
he himself an angry and excited man? – he snatched his
parka and loped flapping out the door in his mukluks
without saying goodbye.

CHAPTER TEN

Outdoors his feet felt cooler at once and he was struck, as always, with the immensity of the blackness. In the face of this nocturnal sky which reversed the claustrophobia of the daytime by opening a hatch for all the giant denizens of space, fear of the dark, ordinary dark, seemed the silliest of phobias, like the fear of feathers. But tonight Alan ignored it and trotted on, eager to catch up with the voices that had drawn him from his house. The shouting was farther away now; he could just see the bobbing flash-lights and lanterns of a dozen men running towards the other end of the village. Light from his own windows and from the other houses scattered ahead of him gleamed on the path at intervals, leaving patches of thicker darkness in between. Alan wished that he had stopped for his flash-light, but to go back now would be to lose the pack up ahead altogether. He decided just to keep his eyes on their lights and try to stay on the path.

The looseness of his mukluks was going to give him a bit of trouble too, he could tell already, and that would increase when his toes got stiff with cold. In the meantime he managed not to slip very much on the packed snow by adopting a peculiar, high-stepping run, like a flat-footed old man's. He was not gaining on the lights, but he was keeping them in sight.

Just at the edge of the village proper, in one of those blacker patches, his right foot struck an obstacle in its upward arc and both feet went out from under him, pitching him headlong onto whatever soft, dense object obstructed his path.

For a moment he floundered and kicked, his senses too surprised at the input to make a coherent report. He was having trouble breathing, both because the wind had been knocked out of him in his fall and because he was face down in some warm, peculiar pocket of sensation that cut off his air. Since he was not in pain he lay still for a moment more, turning his head slightly to the side in its odorous elastic bed, and assessed the situation, still drunk enough to be more curious than alarmed. His torso was lying on something warmer and higher than the snow, but not much wider than he was. His legs trailed off onto the ground on either side of a solid lump which, he now recalled, had just missed giving him a serious thump in a delicate place. But his face – His hair suddenly stiffened with premonition at the back of his neck.

What was so soft and warm and slippery? Whence that metallic taste on his tongue and that odd smell of liver, so unpleasantly reminiscent of dinner? What was undulating across his forehead like his own brains escaped, what was cozying so wetly against his right cheek? He held his breath. It felt like being inside a woman. He patted with his hands at shapes and surfaces. Groping, he remembered the Halloween game; "The witch is dead," whispered the darkness. He tore off his mittens to touch wetness, rough fabric, the teeth of a zipper. God, God, it felt like some place he had no business to be!

Galvanized by unutterable suspicions, he sprang to his feet all in one piece and stood trembling like a spooked animal while he strained his eyes against the night. Beyond doubt, it was a human form that made a darker shape in the blackness, lying the length of the path with its belly ripped open.

Alan uttered one high, inadequate squeal and clawed at his slimy skin before he flung himself off the path to grind his face in the snow. Even in the midst of his passionate revulsion some part of him stepped back briefly and assessed this as the worst moment of his life. He felt too profoundly sick to vomit as he scrubbed and shivered and danced and tried to master his disgust, which at the moment was directed mostly at his own body. He fought an impulse to rip off chunks of his violated flesh and throw them into the dark.

At last his dance slowed. He wiped his sleeve over his face, whimpered once, and stood still. Time had passed; he never afterwards could guess how much. All at once he knew himself to be superficially more calm. He could see the faraway stars and felt his own remoteness while he scrubbed once over the front of his parka for blood, examined the rigidity of his feet, and hobbled off to meet the bobbing lights that were coming nearer again, back from wherever they'd gone. His keenest sensation was a desire to keep secret from all, and forever, the shocking intimacy in which he had unwillingly taken part.

He met the men, still talking and gesticulating among themselves, outside Willie's house where Willie was turning to go in. They looked vexed at seeing him, but tonight Alan didn't mind feeling superfluous to the community. He seemed to see the other men through the wrong end of a telescope while he floated in the void, hugging his shocking secret.

"What happened?" he asked with an affectation of concern, jerking his head back at the path behind him.

"My cousin Louis," Willie said. "He got drunk, beat up his wife. She cut him." Murmurs of assent with a note of outrage arose from the other men. "Martha told him last time, he does it again he's dead. We chased her but she got Louis's snowmobile. Maybe she'll get somewhere before she freezes."

There was a kind of corporate shrug. Even in his detached state Alan thought the men's attitudes curiously ambivalent. They were annoyed that Louis had died for such a humdrum vice as wife-beating, but on the other hand they seemed not to object to the possibility of Martha's escape: such things, like inclement weather, happened.

"Have to fill out papers for the Mounties," Willie sighed as he opened the door. "Triplicate."

Willie's two little boys boiled out onto the path and began to jump like water on a hot skillet in their eagerness to report. They'd been playing with their cousins when the trouble began, and they were pleased and excited. It was they who had run home to spread the alarm when Martha chased Louis outdoors, and swollen with the importance of being witnesses, they could not wait for someone new to tell, and in English besides.

"He hit her with chair, him," they chortled, bouncing from foot to foot. "Big fight. Lots holler. She say she kill him!" Their English was holding up well, Alan thought, knowing they didn't learn it until second grade. "She throw piece meat! He blow nose in curtain! Everybody run, yell. She hit him in eye. He make hole in window. Pick up chair, break on her back!"

The smaller boy capped the linguistic display. "Martha so mad," he giggled, "fire come out her tits!"

Alan looked at him with respect; it was a striking image. After Willie shooed the boys into the house and came back with a tarp for Louis's body, he tagged along at the rear of the group, not so much out of deference as from a desire not to see the corpse again until it was decently covered with canvas. He hadn't known Louis before tonight, though now he felt more closely acquainted with him than his wife, his children, his own mother could have been. He managed to keep his eyes averted after one accidental glimpse of a flashlighted plaid shirt bordering a dark, slippery pit. He was already trying to compose himself to face Diana.

"Well, thanks for the goose," Alan said to Willie, reluctantly disengaging himself from the edge of the gathering. Tasting liver again, he was sorry he'd mentioned it, but he needed to say something friendly that wasn't about Louis.

"Was it good?" Willie asked, polite but a bit astonished.

"Fine," Alan started to say, but gagged a little in the middle of the word and covered it with a cough. He nodded and shuffled off into the darkness that led home.

He walked slowly, trying to sort out his experience before he had to act normal for his wife. His self-pity was mixed with guilt and embarrassment. He didn't want Diana ever to know, but why did he feel so furtive? His state of mind was halfway between that of a man who's had an affair and that of a man who's shit in his pants, with a hint of something less acceptable than either. Well, lying around with your face inside somebody's abdomen is a fearfully intimate thing. That was an intimacy beyond all probability or decency, and the knowledge of Louis's insides had been thrust upon him unwillingly. He recalled vaguely the psychological complications of rape victims and began to believe in them.

As it turned out, Diana was already in bed, though it was still only nine o'clock, and either slept or pretended to sleep. Alan was relieved, both for the privacy it allowed him and because it made him suspect that Diana wasn't really very blithe about their estrangement either. His longing for Diana's love and support hit him with a pang that was almost sweet compared to his earlier detachment and still earlier depression. Emotions began to thaw in the familiar warmth of the house.

In the solitude of the bathroom Alan took off all his clothes, checking them for stains. They were unmarked except for a few smears of blood on the collar of his parka. Hadn't it happened? He must have wiped away the rest in his initial snow-wash, he decided. He cleaned the collar with cold water and blotted it on a towel. It would be dry by morning. Then he quietly washed himself all over at the sink, shampooing his hair and paying especially punctilious attention to all the crevasses of his face and neck. He had not washed his ears so carefully since his last visit, at twelve, to a certain tyrannical great-aunt. When he finished he did not feel especially clean, but he felt safe, like a criminal who has wiped away all his fingerprints.

He slipped into bed beside Diana, lying on his side, facing her back but keeping a careful twelve inches away. That was his custom lately, and the most efficient distance for gathering Diana's smells and sounds and sleeping emanations without her knowing. He was achingly aware of her. What would he not have bargained for that twelve-inch gain tonight when he so needed her against his skin to blot out his necrophilic embrace of Willie's cousin!

Out in the dark, Louis would be stiffening under his canvas. The wetness would be a crackle of ice now, the organs heavy and unreceptive. By morning Louis would be frozen through, lying like a statue fallen from its pedestal. But here in bed Diana's body was still warm. He fought its pull.

Closeness to Diana. The idea throbbed and burned and became the one glowing point of consciousness in his mind while he held his body rigid as Louis's and began to drift. Some time just before he dropped into unconsciousness he found himself lusting to hide his face in Diana's entrails, saw himself sinking through her skin into a pit of colored spirals like the beads on his mukluks, but warm and soft and wet, Diana's core. But he was too sleepy to be shocked.

CHAPTER ELEVEN

Over the following week Alan's revulsion and self-loathing faded, though he still, for other reasons now, kept his experience to himself. Two things from his Christmas day remained vivid: his vision of Cam as a suckling pig and his edge-of-sleep dream about Diana's inner workings. Indeed, they both flourished until their progress caused him to fear for his sanity.

His carnivorous yearning towards Cam was the simpler of the two peculiarities. It had little complication of emotion, being a sensation centered principally in his teeth. Whenever he saw Cam's plump little body, naked or clothed, he was swept with an impulse to snap at one of his limbs. Impulse was perhaps too weak a word. He remembered something like the sensation from his own childhood's teething: he wanted to bite down on something, and the something was Cam. Sometimes he imagined that he was cutting yet another set of teeth, a long wolfish set, and that his horrid thoughts would break out on his face in hairy patches for the whole town to see.

The business about Diana was less movie-monster awful at first, but far more obsessive. There had been thrust upon him a dark vision of intimacy that seemed to answer his appetite for closer union with his wife. At first when he would remember the sensation of being inside Willie's cousin, warm, wet, slippery, enveloping, he would hold off the horror by a quick substitution of Diana for Louis. This made the recollection no longer loathsome. But almost at once the exercise got away from him, and he began to see himself not falling but diving into Diana's belly. The mental flash of himself thrusting his hands and face inside her, wallowing in a bath of visceral delight, never failed to make him shiver with an odd mixture of feelings, among them the undeniably erotic. He saw himself caught up in a caress of tissues more sensitive than hands and spangled with reflected light. After a few days of this, he discovered that his fantasies had shifted again, towards a desire to have Diana inside his own belly. He held at bay a tiny suspicion that the bridge between the two fantasies might have been some vision of organ-eating that his mind had censored.

He tried to work more regularly on the dissertation that he had been neglecting since the Naomi crisis and the subsequent demands of the holiday. Maybe, after all, his odd mental state was the effect of academic guilt and tension, dissertation nerves. Working on any kind of thesis, he knew, could lead to various forms of mild lunacy. He remembered graduate school acquaintances who had broken out in mysterious rashes or fallen in love with altogether unsuitable people, only to recover completely when the last page was typed. Others had flung themselves into eccentric regimens of diet or become accident-prone or found themselves in the grip of compulsive behavior. If only he could emerge from his dissertation with nothing worse than a boring lover or a kitchen full of bean curd, but his case was worse than any he had ever known. Perhaps, he thought, he'd better work faster, both to get through this dangerous period of his life and because work might keep his mind occupied.

It didn't. The blank lines of his yellow pad provoked not a single rational thought. Though he tried to make his task feel real by exploiting the tangibility of its tools – chewing hard on the end of his pen, pressing his diaphragm against the edge of the table – his pain was largely unproductive. The index cards that he shuffled hopefully from time to time slid past his fingers as wraithlike as a stack of transparent gels.

Alan could not decide whether Diana was a worse distraction by her presence or by her absence. She did go out of the house from time to time, for although she seemed not to like him, she was trying to give him time for his work. But Diana out of the way was not out of the way at all; in her absence he was assaulted by the bloodiest and most vivid of his new fancies, which the real Diana in some measure assuaged. Almost as soon as the door shut behind her he would be on his feet pacing, tenderly rapacious dreams beating about his head like gulls. Out-running them was impossible, he discovered, and he was obliged to suffer visions of himself delicately slicing away his wife's flesh or amorously ramming her down his throat, whole and living. Sometimes for the purpose of the latter dream she was mysteriously reduced in size, shrunk by some mad scientist's machine to fifteen inches, a doll-woman who could be dandled and petted and reduced to utter dependency before he swallowed her.

Diana alive and at hand, wrapped in her own selfhood, dispelled the worst of the dreams and made them seem like the half-remembered nightmares generated by dangerously high fevers. But though her presence exorcized, it distracted as well. He would hump over his paper like a spider, feeling her whereabouts in the house send vibrations down the psychic strands he had laid from room to room. He would wait for her to come near him, watching out of the corners of his mind, and make himself sit still when it happened. Sometimes he remembered his college friend who tried to walk through walls and wondered if he could will Diana's molecules to part and pass between his own. If he clasped her to his body and pressed really hard? Could he work the process like his rather modest dreams of flying, where by moving his feet very quickly and holding the right frame of mind he could stay a foot or two off the ground for a hundred yards? It would take only one moment of the right mind set and pressure to put Diana inside his body without his having to devour her.

After nearly a week of tension and incipient breakdown, Alan began to lose appetite as well as energy. Surely nobody had ever been driven so crazy by a dissertation before. Perhaps part of his problem was writing about food distribution. Still, if he was going to go mad, it was no more dangerously provocative than other topics in anthropology – sorcery, incest, sacrifice. He sat at dinner on the sixth night and looked at his bowl of stew as though it were a repugnant curiosity discovered in the stomach of an alien species. Animal flesh. Roots. Seeds. It had nothing to do with him. Diana across the table was spooning it down unperturbed and Cam was at any rate finding it good for finger-painting.

"Cam is getting nice and fat," he observed, and felt a kind of itching ache in his back molars. He ground them together furtively, hoping that he hadn't said anything out of the way.

Diana gazed at the child dotingly and pinched his fat little leg with affection. "Mummy's big boy," she said. Alan was taken aback. So far motherhood had never driven her to the use of fatuous expressions. Poor Diana, it had been a long winter for her too.

The straightforward warmth provoked by that moment

of sympathy told Alan how skewed his recent feelings had been. He had almost forgotten what normal felt like, or maybe he hadn't appreciated it when he had it. Intoxicated with relief, he swung into an old favorite, a safe fantasy in which he peeled off Diana's garments one by one. This was a fine, slow game in Wino Day, where Diana wore many layers of clothing to trap the heat, and he pulled off her outer layers with lazy delight, coming closer and closer to that gem of warmth and good smells and basic pinkness that was Diana underneath. Peel away the cardigan, find the wool turtleneck. Peel away the turtleneck, find the tee shirt a little warmer to the touch, a little more redolent of its owner. But tonight, before he knew what had happened, he had peeled too far, and the phantom Diana who rushed into his outstretched ghostly arms was an anatomist's model of braided muscle, whose skin lay on the floor with the other layers (raw, red lingerie in the lean-to) and whose sensuous entrails spilled into his lap and wrapped themselves around his thighs. He came to with a start.

And as he watched Diana turn his stew into the garbage, holding his chair with both hands lest he fling himself to his knees and sink his teeth into her unsuspecting buttocks, he knew that something would have to be done.

CHAPTER TWELVE

As soon as he began to think of his obsession as something that had to be cured and therefore presumably could be cured, Alan felt a little better. He might after all save his sanity, dissertation notwithstanding. He decided not to worry about his odd attitude towards Cam; that was only a species of unnerving itch. But Diana, whom (if he could bring himself to say it) he wished to consume – there was the problem. The question, he decided after a bout of what he hoped was rational thought, was not so much how to stop having fantasies as how to satisfy his bizarre longings short of uxoricide and cannibalism.

The more he thought about it, the more he felt that the answer must be sexual. No doubt his recent celibacy had contributed to the frantic quality of his mania. He could not quite imagine the means of working off a sexual kink as kinky as his, but in erotic matters the inspiration of the moment may do much.

The chief difficulty was in getting Diana into any sort of sexual situation in her present frame of mind. Surprise attack was out of the question, both because his wife could drop him with a look and because his aspirations were so complicated as to require a good deal of slow experimentation. Persuasion seemed in some ways doomed to failure. The activity once engaged, she would almost certainly cooperate: her "Why shouldn't it be true" attitude had frequently and usefully become, in bed, "Why not give it a try." The trick was getting her to agree to love-making at all. The variety of contemptuous monosyllables with which she might wither a proposition – *"Why?" "Now?" "You?" "Us?" "That?" "Ha!"* – made him so shy before the fact as almost to put him off the project.

Several days passed as Alan weighed the risks of rejection against the risks of growing insanity and hoped that the right moment would announce itself in loud, unmistakable tones. Finally, in a curious way, it did.

It had been a long day, and an empty one. Grey skies, white ground. It was not, Alan had thought, looking out the window for the fifth time in an hour of clutching wilting index cards, that there was so much snow in Wino Day, it was that there was so little else. Diana's civility had made him miss more than ever the old Diana who would curse and argue and kiss and look him in the eye. He had braved his own blood-thirsty impulses to insist on assuming some of Cam's care and feeding, for they not only filled a corner in his enormous boredom but spared him for intervals the sight of the child in Diana's forbidden arms.

When at last he reckoned that he might crawl into his side of the bed and chalk off one more ghastly day, he tiptoed into the bedroom and saw something that drew him up short. Diana was lying in their bed asleep. And so was Cam.

This had never happened before, this nighttime usurpation. At naptime, yes, and that annoyed him enough, Cam and Diana would sometimes lie on top of the bed together under her Aunt Ida's log cabin quilt. But now here was this loud, leaky dwarf of a stranger sprawling all over the No-Man's-Land of the middle and impinging on his private territory as well. Alan could feel the flame of his anger light with a gassy pop. Was Diana getting even for his earlier manoeuvers with Cam? He narrowed his eyes and stared at them through the shadows. Diana's right arm was flung in a curve across the pillows, a shielding gesture that exposed one breast. Cam had fallen asleep at the nipple. And what was that for, anyway? A nightcap? He'd had his feeding at dinner. Or was it some kind of erotic goddam thing? He'd show them erotic. One for the road, Cam! He thought he could feel the fires break out behind his pupils.

With the tense deliberateness of the criminally insane, he plucked off his garments and dropped them around his feet. With stealthy care he reached across the empty half of the bed and lifted Cam straight up into the air, aware that it shouldn't be possible, not easily, and carried him like eggs across the room. Cam never stirred. Alan wanted to bite him (he saw himself shapechanging into a werewolf father and tearing at the child's flesh). He also wanted to throw him across the room. But both desires paled beside his need for Cam to arrive silently in his own crib. Cam's bed was not turned down, evidence that Diana had meant to keep him beside her all night, and Alan slipped the blankets away from under his still-sleeping child to spread them over him.

Feeling that all things were possible now, he crept into bed without joggling Diana and began to inch his way across the mattress. At his old twelve-inch line he paused, feeling an almost palpable barrier. Habit, or the woman, was making strong vibes. Pushing through it, he permitted himself a small celebratory smile on credit. Weren't the sheets warmer inside it, more aromatic, tingling with sweet static? He slid as close as he could get without touching her. Very cautiously then he shifted his position, stretching out his tongue to meet Diana's nipple. So great was the psychic distance still that he seemed to reel it out of his mouth like cable. The sudden hint of milk on his taste buds cheered him with visions of accomplished intimacy, and with a catch in his breath he took up Cam's position, closing his lips around the nipple and venturing to stroke her far side with his convex palm, hardly daring to put his fingers down. The milky taste delighted him not so much in itself as because it had come from her hidden inner workings. But in this he had no more than Cam had.

He knew that soon Diana would sense his mouth to be too big, too toothy, too whiskery for Cam's, and be startled. In fact, she had better sense it soon, or his jealousy would take a lively new turn. She was *his*, never Cam's. And that damned Cam had by Alan's own contrivance been farther inside her than he could go. (But not farther than he had gone into Louis.) He would find a way, he had to find a way, to make Diana a part of his body. In the meantime, however, he revelled in the hot satin touch of her skin and made little expeditions of sensation. He unreeled his tongue again to lick the salty declivity between her breasts and laid his ear to her rib cage. Muffled sounds of activity led him farther down the abdomen, an impenitent eavesdropper. Once he imagined that he heard fireworks and the sound of cheering. Partying, and he had not been invited! He would have peered through her navel if he could have.

She stirred and moved against him as he stroked her thigh with his trembling hand. She was waking up. "Honey?" he whispered, sliding back up, "You awake?" He felt his panic mount. Her answering mumble triggered a barrage of pleadings, explanations. He knew himself to be incoherent. Now, please, it had been so long, he loved her, he adored her, she knew that, he'd be careful, he wanted, he needed, could he just try. Through one slitted eye she gave him a glance compounded of lassitude and sensuality, shrugged, and lay still. To a married man the shrug was eloquent: "As long as it feels good, but don't expect any help." Though he felt that her primary motive was to shut him up, he was more than content.

In his gladness he pulled her whole body against his, running his hands swiftly up and down her back in his greed to have all of her. For a moment, as he pulled her groin to his, he hoped for a magical interpenetration. Flesh met flesh and stopped. He paused, holding her ass now with less conviction, to calculate strategy.

He felt for the first time that his penis was constructed on the wrong principle. This was a shock. He had always been pleased with it, and in his more foolish youth as fatuously conceited as if he had invented it himself. He had even considered giving it one of those pet names by which his peers were conferring upon their organs a useful moral autonomy, but in the end, gazing down at it and considering what name would fit, he had been put off by the inconsistency of christening that but not his other appendages. And now this heretofore inspired piece of anatomical engineering was useless to his purposes, for it only put out, and he needed something that would draw in; he needed it to work like the hose of an enormously powerful industrial vacuum cleaner, pulling Diana into his body. If he put it in her and turned it on, could she not be sucked inside out like a pink silk stocking and rearranged under his own skin, stretched so that her fingers fit inside his fingers, her knees cupped into his own, and her nipples charged his from behind like the positive ends of two dry cell batteries?

Diana made a barely audible noise that he understood to express impatience and growing boredom. "Come on, Kirby," he whispered to his penis, remembering that to name a thing gives one power over it, but no little motors started up. Christened or no, it stood there dull and dispassionate as a sausage.

His initial elation rapidly giving way to the premonition of failure, he resumed sucking and nibbling, moving from her breast up her neck. Was her acquiescence, having come so offhandedly, worth anything? Did she know herself so safe inside her packaging that she could afford to let him fumble at the surface? He took one ear inside his mouth, entire, and rubbed his teeth across its base, poking with his tongue around its spirals. Such a little opening; could he suck her brain through it bit by bit, like the yolk of an egg? If he had that, would he have the quintessential Diana? All the human orifices were so damned *small* – how could he get in, or better yet, coax her out? While his mind spun, his hands were racing over her body with a fervor less sexual than exploratory. The Lady Isabella, groping for Otranto's trap door in the dark, knew something of his desperation.

There was no name for the kind of thing he wanted, no name at least in the lexicon of erotica. "Federated" came into his mind as he mouthed Diana's kneecap, and he remembered fleetingly a political cartoon from the archives at Vic. A small chicken labelled Victoria University had been eaten by a large chicken hawk called The University of Toronto. "Oh, he's been federated," somebody said to explain the chicken's disappearance. Only Alan was not on the cartoonist's side but the hawk's, for what should be a simple marital union was not, for him, enough. Nothing was enough. Only in dreams could he federate a whole Diana by cramming her down his throat.

Mechanically, sadly now, he continued to move around and around her body, sucking this, cupping that, burrowing at the other. "Let me in," he whispered once with his cheek against her skin, but he didn't really expect a response. He had known from the first that ordinary oral sex was no use, but he gave it a pass from time to time on his way by, a perfunctory nod to yesterday's pleasures. He felt like a hungry man who owns a can of sardines but no key, or a child trying to lick a shrink-wrapped lollipop. He felt helpless. What was he to do? Though he had licked every texture and tongued every orifice, though he had pressed for secret panels and sliding doors, though he had gagged himself in an ill-conceived ambition to swallow her toes, her body in the final analysis proved as seamlessly inaccessible as her spirit. He perceived himself a fool as well as a madman.

No species of sex, however ingenious, he acknowledged regretfully, answered his peculiar needs. Really, sex had never been close enough for what he wanted, and now that he conceived true intimacy to be the conjunction of internal organs, not the juxtaposition of skins, he knew that the erotic solution was hopeless.

It came to him all at once that Diana had been uncommonly unresponsive for some time, as well (in all fairness) she might. How could he apologize for her boredom? Hoping to placate her with some abject words and a goodnight kiss, he raised his head to look at her face. As he lay back down and wept tears of dejection into her pubic hair, he wondered how long she had been asleep.

Because Alan rather hoped that Diana would, if she remembered them at all, remember his ludicrous attempts
of the night before as a dream, he was up early, whistling
over the oatmeal pot and looking vehemently natural. He
tried to gauge the success of his nonchalance, but Diana
was so withdrawn, so closed in upon herself, that his furtive glances at her face told him nothing. At least she did
not mention the incident, or, he thought sadly, the non-
incident.

So, sexual invention was not the solution. It had
seemed so promising, too, perhaps because the intensity
of his need resembled lust more closely than anything else
he knew. How, then, was he to manage his craziness?

As the days passed – only a few days, he thought afterwards in surprise when he looked at a calendar – his
difficulties multiplied. Time had fallen out of its natural
rhythm for him, so that days sometimes seemed like weeks

and sometimes ran together like one long, interminable, sleepless day. "Perish in his slow-chapt power," he kept saying to himself, proud to think that in a crisis he kept his grip on Lit 271, but his vision of tiny men and women crushed in the leisurely, inexorable molars of Time came too near his own lunacy and had to be fought away.

Struggles to objectify his plight by reviewing different cultural concepts of time passage did no good, so one more protection was gone – the anthropologist's greatest personal reward, the ability to push back his own troubles and see them in a broader context. He felt vulnerable, with neither the breastplate of scholarship nor the practiced elasticity of his Indian neighbors. He knew that he could be broken, exploded, driven altogether mad.

He might even starve, he thought. His excuses for eating little or nothing would never have passed with a caring wife who was paying attention. True, he wanted to keep secret his dreadful changes, but he wanted also to flaunt them like a beggar's sores and elicit sympathy in this crisis of his mental health. Once, pushing his fish and tinned peas around his plate, fearing to look up lest his eyes spill over with tears of self-pity, he remembered his father sitting just so, poking at his dinner to cover his alcoholic aversion to food. For a moment he almost thought he was at home in his parents' house. He seemed to see his mother's lace tablecloth instead of their oilcloth, to hear the cicadas instead of the stove. He remembered the green and dusty leaves of the hydrangea outside the dining room window, the sound of the older boys hot-rodding up the street, the thundery smell of summer in the midwest.

More poignant even than his sudden longing for the home he had more than half despised was his recollection that he had always been impatient because he wanted to run out and join his friends. They would have some ex-

cursion or project at hand, and he would be trapped in
that room while his father, who he knew full well would
not and could not eat, impeded Alan's own affairs by pretending to. *He had wanted to do something*, there was the
sore place, and it had been something innocent, something to be done in the green outdoors in the sight of his
companions. How warm and big-skyed and open his life
must have been then, how ordinary his desires. Though in
recent years his objects had only been the needling lusts
of academia and his grasping love for his wife, even those
fell within the purlieu of normality. But now, now, all his
desires were salty-red and secret, the kind of desires that
come to fruition only in the dark icy rooms of snow-lapped
cabins when all color is gone from land and lives, and the
sun itself makes the most perfunctory of visits.

Oddly, the growth of his madness brought certain kinds
of relief. A man in constant pain is spared the onset of
pain after respite. Alan no longer dreaded the attack of
his fantasies, for they were always with him. Further, the
cloud of craziness around him widened to take in others
outside his household. Diana was still the nucleus of his
longing, because she mattered to him. But Cam, who had
never really mattered very much except as a living sign, in
the hospital nursery, of his manhood, now looked not sig-
nificantly more toothsome than the children of his
neighbors. Though he had been shocked at his first wolfish response to the village women and children, it now
sustained him to some degree. Less intense than his lust
for Diana, it offered a sorry recreation when he was driven
out by the temptations of his own home.

He would slip along the paths of the village, feeling
hairily lean-shanked and loping, reminding himself not to
let his tongue loll out between his great white teeth. "Alan
the wolfman," he said to himself, "Alan the midnight
shadow, making the blackness blacker." For the first time

he felt superior to his neighbors in cunning and adaptability. "Can't catch me," he whispered in his head as he appraised the scabby but nevertheless acceptable arms of underclad preschoolers trotting between the houses; "Can't even *see* me," he jeered as he mentally nibbled the flesh from the finger bones of Mrs. Dantouze reaching out for her mail. "Go boil old ladies," he shouted silently at the back of Naomi's daughter Elizabeth, thinking that he could bring her down with four long quadruped lopes and a spring to the neck, "but you won't boil *me*!" "Windigo, windigo," he chanted experimentally to himself, liking the free sound of it, "go like the wind, like the wind I go." Though in fact all his own cultural background inclined him to see himself more as a werewolf.

When he came home from his snowy prowls he would feel better for a little while, though embarrassed. Then he might sit for as much as an hour, plaguing his wife's remoteness with small talk and suspending any craving for more than the superficial.

Sometimes in his moments of comparative lucidity he contemplated a third theory, monotony of diet. It seemed an inadequate explanation but perhaps at least as a compounding factor he had some dietary deficiencies or frustrations. Maybe his boredom with Wino Day food drove him to forbidden appetites. He remembered that people with dietary deficiencies ate all kinds of weird things – laundry starch, mud. One of his graduate professors had told him once, over a beer, about a childhood contemporary in London, Ontario, who could not be restrained from dashing into the street at the sound of hooves to eat fresh horse shit. There was no logical connection between lack of fresh vegetables and the desire for human meat, but if one's frustration at the lack of bagels and artichokes and eggnog and Big Macs and peaches and English muffins and hard salami should rise unconsciously, while one was not looking, to fever pitch – well, perhaps one would be seized with some kind of angry omnivorousness.

Thus his days. His nights were marked by fitful sleep and stressful but unremembered dreams. He stayed more willingly on his own side of the bed now, wanting Diana but wanting also to wrap his body around his private lunacy to protect it while he slept. He often, though not always, turned his back to her now.

One night in the depths of January his dreaming took a new turn. Like everything else in his life (except permissible food), the shapes in Proxene's drawings looked compellingly edible. No brooms this time, for who would want to brush aside such manna? No skates either. Flat on his stomach, Alan wriggled and drifted like his prey, become by his hunger as two-dimensional and toothy as they. But he didn't think much about his own metamorphosis (after all, dreamers don't), he just swam along, trying in vain to slide his lower jaw like a spatula under those tantalizing, elusive shapes. A lucky taste or two had proven their substance ephemeral as cotton candy but more satisfying. Trouble was, their shapes kept changing. Just as he bit at a round cookie shape it would shift into the no-less-tempting likeness of a human leg, and Alan would snap his jaws shut six inches from the back of a bent knee. His hunger and frustration mounted while eggs concaved into chops, perch narrowed into eels, and one aggressively pink breast changed to clutching fingers that nearly had *him* as he lunged into the opening by the thumb. He wriggled faster. At last the plane of the drawing dipped ahead of him, and he began to see that if he could come at a shape from above, sink his teeth into the middle of it, he'd win no matter how unstable its edges. At the crest of the dip he hung for a moment, eyeing a succulent blue oval, and dived on it.

His yell of triumph rose unmuffled by the sweetness

that crammed his mouth, and then something struck him heavily across the face. The dream film flickered. Stop the action. It took a moment for the horror of his waking situation to catch up with him. Diana was crouching on the far corner of the bed in the darkness, weeping and cursing and clutching her shoulder. Alan groped for the light as Cam added his shrieks to the general pandemonium.

"You bit me, you asshole," Diana yelled. "You get away from me!"

"Mummee," Cam was screeching as he beat at his prison. Diana backed to the crib and snatched Cam up like a weapon, which in some senses he was.

Alan felt unmasked to his marrow. He knew the utter hopelessness of the apprehended pickpocket, the kid caught beating off under the bleachers, the crone floating to the top of the ducking pond. Had he talked as well as bitten? Could Diana fail to recognize the scope of his madness and incipient criminality?

Apparently she could, though she regarded him with anger and loathing. "You're not getting back in *this* bed," she said. "Take your goddam eating dreams out to the kitchen for the night." Saved! This was merely that rage stimulated by pain that would sometimes make her kick shin-bruising objects across the room to teach them a lesson. Nothing, in fact, would have induced him to share sleep or mattress with her after such a dangerous faux pas as biting her shoulder, so he dug out his sleeping bag and went off into the kitchen mumbling apologies. It was three a.m.

Alan lay on the hard floor, contemplating his reprieve and listening to Diana quieting Cam in their bed. Her bed. He could not trust himself any more, awake or asleep, he admitted now. He would take no more chances. He shifted his bones against the floor, and turned over and over all his possible routes of escape until at last, satisfied, he fell into a wary doze.

CHAPTER FOURTEEN

Diana woke him up by stepping over his sleeping bag on her way to the stove. It was morning, evidently. It felt like the mornings of dentist appointments, maybe even the mornings of funerals. Behind her back Alan ducked into the bathroom to delay any confrontation. He was surprised that he still showed in the shaving mirror, but he did – red-eyed, whiskery, pouchy-faced. Was that how were-wolves looked the morning after? His own joke failed to amuse him, for he felt all too human.

He brushed his teeth three complete times. He washed behind his ears twice. He shaved more carefully than he had since his wedding day. Finally, straightening his backbone, trying to swallow, wishing that he was accustomed to prayer, he emerged. "I'm sorry," he said, feeling helpless, as he got his own coffee and sat down across from Diana and Cam.

"You didn't do it on purpose." Her voice was peculiar, not unkind but coiled, perhaps, to spring at the wrong gesture from him. Her face, too, was somehow alien. Transparent was the only word he could think of, like resin or ice, but of course that wasn't quite right. Certainly he couldn't see through her in the figurative sense, and she was, strictly speaking, opaque, but she did seem made of some substance other than flesh. It seemed to him incredible that he had ever been of one mind or one body with this lovely, inimical stranger.

"I've been thinking," Alan said, clearing his throat, "that I should go to Toronto for a little while." Diana looked startled, then inscrutable. "No need for you and Cam to come," he went on according to plan, "no need to disrupt Cam's routine. After all, it's not exactly the Bahamas there in January. I can just crash with a friend if I'm alone."

"Unless of course you want to go?" he stammered, hoping she didn't. Her eyes told him nothing.

It was absolutely crucial, he had decided during his hours on the kitchen floor, to get away by himself until he got over his insanity, lest he do his wife or child an injury. It was equally crucial, given their current estrangement, that he go off for such plausible reasons that his return would be taken for granted. Toronto was not the nearest point of refuge, Winnipeg would have been easier, but their connections to Toronto offered excuses. To be sure, Toronto had its dangers, for friends still lived there whom he would not wish to see until (he could not bear to say "unless") he was better, and nothing would have been more normal than to take Diana and Cam there for a break from Wino Day, to which his whim and no one else's had consigned them all.

He went on with his story. "You know I've been kind of stuck with the dissertation." That at any rate was true enough. "Well, I've finally realized that I'm up against a major contradiction in my evidence and I don't think I should go on until I talk to my supervisor." Did she know how flimsy that sounded? "And I'll probably have to do a little research there, too, so I might be gone a few days."

Diana scraped Cam's last bite of cereal off his chin and poked it into his mouth. Alan thought briefly that Cam should be feeding himself by now. Hadn't he been doing it for a little while? Why wasn't Diana reacting? He plunged on.

"I guess," he added, "that while I'm there I'd better go to the dentist for a checkup. My teeth have been feeling a little funny lately." That line had been unwise; he choked back a giggle on its way to a sob. Why hadn't he quit at the academic excuse? Until Diana reacted he found it hard to stop talking, that was why. He dreaded her silence.

"I can bring back supplies," he said. He tried to think of the names of food but his stomach lurched, so he added, "Something nice."

"So go," Diana said calmly. She stood up with Cam and walked off clucking into his neck.

Alan was nonplussed. His stories had been so carefully worked out, and now it seemed that he could have packed and left without her looking up as he closed the door behind him. "Don't let the door hit you in the ass on your way out," that had been the way his father used to express contemptuous dismissal. Didn't Diana even envy him at all for going (as they now called it) South? Was going with him too high a price to pay, perhaps? Ordinarily nothing could have induced him to leave her with so virulent an estrangement in progress, but he was doing it for her own safety. He tried to hearten himself with visions of his nobility, but he found them poor encouragement. It's hard to think of yourself as noble when you've spent half the night on the floor as punishment for biting your sleeping wife.

He packed in silence and wiped his eyes once or twice on a clean shirttail. He would get a seat on the afternoon flight to Thompson and then wait in Gwyn River as long as necessary to catch a plane to Winnipeg, and do it again from Winnipeg to Toronto. At the last moment he remembered to throw in a handful of index cards, snatched up absolutely at random.

Twenty-two hours after he boarded the little Otter to fly out of Wino Day he walked onto a plane headed for Toronto. He considered that he might have done much worse. He found his seat, blessedly beside a stringy-looking old man in a cowboy hat, and belted himself in with a sense of thankfulness for even that restraint. Diana and Cam had come to the airstrip to see him off, and Diana had explained to the child that they'd come again when Daddy's plane brought him back. Alan was touched by even so obliquely positive a gesture.

He had thought of staying in Winnipeg when he got that far, but for a number of reasons had not done so. The sight of so many people in the airport unnerved him after the isolation of the previous months. That would be no better in Toronto, of course, but the impulse to immediate flight was strong. Besides, he knew his way around Toronto and he loved the place. Being there would be just a bit of compensation for everything else, though the memory of his time there with Diana would be saddening. Then too, Winnipeg's freestanding ads for fishing lodges ($1000 a week) made him feel the wilderness still too close. The farther from the perils of Wino Day he moved, the more his spirits lifted. Even looking down at his wife and child on the ground and grieving at their loss, he had felt a kind of freeing. Toronto would be best.

In Toronto, if he went at last hopelessly mad and gave in to his hungers, he would not be killing and eating his own family at least. They would be safe from him, and he would never recover sanity to find that he had destroyed what he loved most (or second most by a large margin, if it were Cam). Besides that, a city may offer anonymity to a crazed killer with any discretion, Alan thought wryly. If the impulse was too strong, perhaps he could grab somebody quietly and never be caught, just bundle the body home, even cook it if he had kitchen privileges. Couldn't he just slip down to Dundas and snatch up an unattended Chinese toddler? Chinese child cooked with water chestnuts and pea pods! It sounded so hideously good that he nearly tasted it and he rushed on in an effort to convince himself that he'd been joking – mission bum marinade, graduate student stewed in its own ink. He had almost felt his teeth meet in that tender saffron flesh, and he was hungry, dreadfully hungry, for all his aversion to food.

When at last he looked out the window of the plane and saw Toronto's welcoming lights – so many of them! – on the edge of the lake, he remembered that he had no place to go. He did not plan to carry his disease, whatever it was, into the apartments of his old friends. Further, it had become increasingly evident during his trip that he was on the verge of illness. He was weak, shaky, possibly feverish, and only by giving airport lunch counters a wide berth had he avoided retching. No one anywhere in the world loved him enough to help him through this dangerous and unattractive malady, he was certain; he had always hoped, to be sure, that Diana would cherish him in any straits, but there was no deluding himself now. He would so cheerfully have nursed her through leprosy, typhoid, delirium tremens, and bubonic plague that he had been almost sorry for her good health. He permitted himself an audible sigh at the memory of her beautiful, impassive face in its hooded parka as she turned it up to the departing plane and waved Cam's hand. His seatmate threw him a look of mistrust.

Alan began to cast about in his mind for cheap and impersonal accommodation. The question had never come up when he lived there. He had a dim recollection, at last, of a YMCA not far from the University. On Spadina, he thought. That would do. He had never set foot in it, but it sounded right. He could take the subway there from the airport. Or was it, on second thought, at Bay? He hoped not. Bay was too near the heart of the bustle. He would get out at Spadina in any case and see what happened.

By the time he got off the plane, his knees were shaking in earnest and he felt like shrieking at the shock of brightness, speed, masses of people. It was much worse than Winnipeg. Was this the feeling that the other whites had called being "bushy" – the inability to readjust at first to modern civilization? Somehow, veering and cringing, his back to the wall as much as possible, he found his way to the bus that went to the closest end of the subway line. Somehow at Islington he steeled himself to leap from the solid platform into the rib cage of that swift, snaky vehicle that he felt he had not seen for twenty years at least. Because he got on at the end of the line he was sure of a seat, at any rate. He could not have stood up even by wrapping himself around a pole.

He shut his eyes until he got used to the motion of the train. One sensation at a time, please. At last he ventured to look around him. It was not so bad. Eight other people, five of whom looked unnervingly urban but not threatening, that was all, and eight was not more than he could tolerate. Still, he removed his glance from the two Oriental businessmen, for they reminded him of his mental lapse on the plane. He began to read ads, trying to skip over the ones for food – what a lot of those there were – and read the ones for pantyhose, though they depressed him a bit. He had been avoiding the ad with the red maple leaf directly across from him, for he was certain that it had to do with groceries. Yes indeed, he perceived at last, it was a Dominion ad. (Could he face a supermarket? It would be a goal, certainly.) The slogan sprang at him like an accusation – "Mainly Because of the Meat."

Not fair, he protested, shutting his eyes again. Nobody else's weaknesses were emblazoned on the wall. Nobody else was pointed out. Though of course it would be funny if somebody else in the car *was* feeling the same way. Then it would be one of these signs like "Uncle Sam Wants YOU" or "The Eye of the Eternal is Upon You." He made up other slogans to keep his mind busy. Message of the day – "The IRS knows"; "Check your armpits"; "Your teacher has already called home"; "Where is your wife tonight?"

The last of these failed to entertain. He began instead to count stops until Spadina. Seven more, lucky number? High Park, Keele, Dundas West, Lansdowne, Ossington, Christie, Bathurst. He recited the names like an incantation to keep his mind clear. Some of them he knew. High Park – he and Diana had gone there one prematurely springy day and rowed on Grenadier Pond and fed the ducks. They'd stopped for tea afterwards. It had been lovely. From Ossington you could see the gold domes of the Ukrainian Catholic church and the shops had an ethnic flavor. They'd bought her aunt a piece of Russian lacquerware there the last Christmas she'd been alive, a slim cylindrical jar of uncertain use, but gorgeous. A light snow had been falling and they had laughed immoderately about something which he now forgot. At Bathurst the station was complicated with trolley tracks and you got off for Honest Ed's, where they'd gone for cheap toasters and mattress pads and lamp shades, the minimal domestic appointments. Maybe when he felt better, if he did, he'd get off there and walk down Markham Street again. That was nice even in January with its trees and streetlights. Maybe he'd get Diana a big gaudy movie poster at Welcome to Yesterday.

Spadina was the next stop. Journey's end. He had a sudden understanding, as he began the extraordinarily long flight of stairs up to the east side of the street (farther from Wino Day), shoulder against the tiled wall for support, that it was journey's end indeed, for if he did not cure himself in the next couple of weeks he would either die or disgrace himself past redemption. Luckily two students took pity on his state and held the glass doors at the exit open until he could tremble through.

CHAPTER FIFTEEN

Alan stood shaking against the outer wall of the subway station. He had set his suitcase down but kept it between his feet from a sudden terror, wholly unsupported by any previous experience in this city, that he might be set upon by brigands who would maim and kill for a chance at his clean socks or index cards. He peered down Spadina, try-ing not to be disoriented by the sweeping headlights, and thought that he saw the building he remembered, on the southwest corner of the intersection. The wrong side of the street, dammit. He would have to cross twice. God, but there were a lot of cars on Spadina below Bloor – lanes and lanes of them, and all so fast! Would they really stop for the light? Could he get across? He would have to try, for the night was cold with a biting wind all the way from Lake Ontario at the bottom of the city, and he was getting no stronger.

"Pull yourself together," he found himself saying out loud. "If you can't cross the street alone, how will you handle the rest of it?" It was a good question, so he moved carefully to the corner and poised himself at the curb, his back to the Canadian Imperial Bank of Commerce and his face to the Bank of Montreal. He struggled for some grim witticism about rivers and the opposite bank, but it was beyond him; he couldn't even remember the name of the river that runs through Hades.

Crossing the street with the light, he felt encouraged. It was going better than he had expected. The march across Bloor was worse, but not impossible. And really, Toronto was not cold at all compared to Wino Day. He almost wished that he had brought Diana and Cam; maybe he would recover quickly from the mere change of environment. Then he remembered again with a dropping of the heart that Diana was not at present his friend.

On the southwest corner he was given further scope for despair. The building was dark. His recollection had been good, but not good enough – bad to the tune of one letter, in fact. An unsympathetic metal H, where there should have been a C, told him that he had found the Young Men's Hebrew Association. More rejection. If only it were open, he mourned, standing in the wind, and he a young Hebrew. God, but he would associate. Of course, if he really were, he would never be in this fix; his high-handed Jewish mother would have taken better care of him. He'd be safe in bed right now with a bowl of hot chicken cliché, getting well. And the YMHA looked so solid, modern, unimaginative. How erotic could a person's fantasies get, inside those blocky walls? But, alas, he himself could not get inside them either.

Perhaps, then, the Y was at Bay? And what could the intersecting street be? He'd ask when he got a chance. At any rate, shaky or not, he would walk south, away from Bloor. That would be quieter. The block to the right was still and shadowy, a good place for a pervert to skulk along. A good place for him.

Farther down Spadina he could see another pedestrian, someone coming from a side street and passing under a streetlight. It looked like a woman. Alan tried to hurry lest he lose her, but she came on steadily. She walked, he observed, like someone who knew her directions. He'd ask her. Indeed, she was a better walker than he, and met him well before he'd reached the second intersection.

"Excuse me," he croaked, and tired, shrewd eyes looked up to assess him. There was no apprehension of strangers in the woman's self-possessed glance, merely appraisal. She reminded him a little of Naomi, but he could not have placed her age within twenty years. "I was looking for the Y," he said. "To stay at."

"Yes," she said, considering. "Yes, that would be very wise." She shifted her briefcase and pointed. "I should go across Harbord and down through the park to College, then east on College." Another weighing up. "There are benches," she added pointedly.

Alan was so undone by her concerned scrutiny that he opened and closed his mouth in silence several times. He greatly wished to gabble all his problems to this bright-eyed stranger, for he thought that he had seldom seen a kinder face. He was checked by imagining what she would say to his story; "You are most unwise," she would say, perhaps, and snap that decisive mouth shut, and he would be judged forevermore. So he shuffled a little, thanked her, and began to move away. He thought he heard her murmur to herself, as he turned, "For life is thorny and youth is vain." He didn't recognize the quotation but he hoped she meant "futile." The encounter had given him some notion of how bad he must look, as well as a faint hope that Toronto would nurture him.

The subsequent details of his feverish and furtive nine-block journey to the Y he could never afterwards recall, except that once he rested in the park, gazing up at the equestrian statue, wishing he had a horse, and watching the spiral effect of wet branches in front of streetlights. And at last he found himself on College, just before Bay. On his right the old Hospital for Sick Children loomed smoky-red and Gothic. On his left the steps and pillars of the YMCA promised a roof and a place to lie down, if not the reassuring modernity of the Young Men's Hebrew Association.

A quarter of an hour later he shut his door with relief and stretched out on his bed. He looked around him. The room was neither luxurious nor modern, but it was sanctuary. He began to feel a little of the nobility he had been unable to call up before he left Wino Day. However much his obsessions might be his own fault, the result of flaws or inadequate resistance or basic craziness, he had managed to go away and put his family out of danger. He was still worth something as a human being.

His watch told him that it was only 8:20. He would take a shower and consider the situation. Padding down the hall to the shower room, he felt that he had got a second wind. His knees shook hardly at all, and the hot water needling over his body gave him several moments of actual pleasure. Again he felt a little hopeful. Perhaps Diana's coldness had made him worse than he had needed to be. Perhaps coming away from her was safer for him as well. That thought was uneasy company, for he had been building his life around the assumption that she was nothing but good for him. He squashed the idea by pointing out to himself that his craziness had begun after his Christmas night experience (actually he thought of it as Experience with a capital E) and that Diana at any rate had not been responsible for its extraordinary loathsomeness, which seemed to have set off the whole business.

Back in his room and dressed in a clean shirt, same jeans, he began to worry about food. Hunger was going to be an issue, as was physical strength. He had not noticed his weakness so much in Wino Day, where he moved around relatively little, and besides, the condition was progressive. Really he had only picked at his food for two or three weeks now, and he had looked scrawny in the Y shower. He considered making his way back up to Bloor, to some unpretentious lunchroom or grill. But could he in fact make it before his second wind, which he suspected would be brief, gave out? And what if he was sick in the restaurant, or unable to eat any of the food he ordered? Feeling incapable of facing disgusted waitresses and other customers in his condition, he gave up the notion of going out.

Perhaps he could order something in. Was it permissible? He had never stayed in a Y before and had no idea. But the cafeteria on the first floor was closed, he had noticed when he checked in, so he'd have to try it. What had he and Diana used to have delivered? It was so long since he'd done it. There was Chinese food, of course, but that had too many psychic ramifications at the moment. There was pizza. He hadn't had a fresh pizza for months, he remembered. Broth seemed more in his line, but perhaps he could eat a pizza just because it was such a change, so spicy, so unlike flesh in all its textures. It would be quite free from disturbing associations.

From the pay phone downstairs he placed his order for one large pizza. Mushroom and pepperoni was his favorite kind, though he doubted the wisdom of the pepperoni. On the verge of ordering plain mushroom he decided that he could pick off the pepperonis and flush them down the toilet if he didn't want them, while the familiar combination just might spur his appetite to normal behavior.

He hung around downstairs and stared through the heavy front doors while he waited for the pizza truck. The lights and traffic astounded him, though he knew in his rational part that College Street was not exactly the Great White Way. At this rate he'd have to put off the gaudy excitements of Yonge Street's neon for quite some while. So here he was. Was it really the same he who had loped around an Indian community by another lake, thinking carnivorous thoughts? The same man who twenty-four hours earlier would have cut off one of his own personal hands for a reconciliation with an ice-woman called Diana? Less fantastic now but equally remote was the Alan who had suffered the torments of adolescent boredom in the midwest. Ah, Boredom, old buddy, Alan thought: come live with me and be my love and I'll never mean-mouth you again.

The pizza, when it came, smelled formidable. How could a man feel so hungry and so queasy at the same time? Alan rushed it to his room and shut the door with his foot. Then he set the box on his writing table and whipped back the cover, turning his face to avoid the first rush of steam. A fight to the death: would he attack that great red saucer and swallow it, or would it rout him and send him away retching? Man vs. Pizza, an epic battle. He giggled a little and decided to assault. And in this corner, he said to himself, Alan Hooper wearing his sleeves pushed up. He stood over the thing and grabbed a slice, which he bolted as fast as he could, not really chewing it, just breaking it up with his teeth. Before he could lose his impetus he shoved a second slice after it.

They came back so swiftly and with so little fanfare that Alan stood for a moment staring down at the fragments now decorating Luigi's Best along with the mushrooms and pepperonis and felt confused. The pieces were so little the worse for wear that he felt as though he were the victim of a cinematographic trick, as though his bit of film had just been re-run backwards. Acute sensations of nausea followed – was this like the theory that first you run and then you feel frightened? – but his flopping stomach was empty. Well, he thought, he had apparently demon-strated that he couldn't yet eat pizza, and in any case its state discouraged a second try.

But what was he to do with the damned thing? He had rather meant to present any leftovers to the desk clerk, who had winked at him encouragingly, but a puked-on pizza is, properly speaking, no longer bestowable. He cast a quick eye around his room for inspiration. The waste-basket was out of the question. He could smell it in there and would dry-heave all night. Down the toilet was out of the question. The thing was rigid and even if he could bear to handle the slices separately they would ruin the plumbing and he would be caught. He began to feel as though he had a body to dispose of. (That, he thought, he might have managed to get down. Though of course there were the bones. He remembered once seeing an old man on the subway with a paper shopping bag full of large clean bones. That intrigued him now.) There was the box, too, also repellent to him. He knew from experience that even if he could find an incinerator slot the box wouldn't fit down it. He hadn't the strength to bend it. His windows, which he tried after establishing that they faced away from the street, would not open, at least not for him. Could he put the pizza under the mattress like groom's cake under the pillow? And what in hell would he dream about then?

With a sudden burst of genius he moved the box with its nasty contents onto the floor, emptied his suitcase hel-ter-skelter onto the table, and shoved box, pizza, puke, and all into his suitcase, which he slammed shut and locked. Well, he had vanquished the thing even if he hadn't eaten it; he had defiled and imprisoned it. He would win after all, for he was resourceful and inde-pendent. Tomorrow he really would have to find something he could eat, he told himself, but in the mean-time — Without undressing, he lay down on the bed and fell into a dreamless sleep.

Though he had chosen an unpretentious little super-market, he panicked for a moment outside the doors. Would it be too much for him? It was better than those tiny one-man groceries at any rate, for it would provide more aisles in which he might collapse, if it came to that, with relative privacy. He could wander unobserved, seeking what he might devour. But how the place was full of food and people! At least he could begin to make a distinction between the two, he comforted himself. He had eaten nothing since he left Wino Day. It was time. If he had to, he could apply the seasick remedy and keep poking food down until it stopped coming up. But how unwell he felt and how unsteady his legs were. He would go in and lean on a cart.

Pushing through the glass doors, he was astounded at the colossal odor of food that assaulted his nose despite all the plastic wrapping. Even the vegetable section hit him a powerful whack. It had been a long time since he had smelled fresh vegetables in quantity. He acquired a grocery cart, draped himself over its handle, and began to cripple down the first aisle past the greenery. How very lush and aggressive it looked, the carrots viciously pointed at one end, the escarole shooting its foliage about, the artichokes all spiky. The fruit looked less hostile. Round is not a very threatening shape, so Alan tentatively chose an orange, one orange, and laid it in the farthest corner of his basket, where he could smell it least. Vitamin C should do him some good, and if he could not bring himself to eat it, he might suck the juice. He felt, although ill, rather pleased with himself as he pushed the cart on.

At the back wall he found himself facing straight into a refrigerated rack of Melton Mowbray pork pies. He almost gave up right then, doubling into his cart with his nose dangerously near his orange as some physical or psychic pain stabbed his innards. Incredible that he used to like pork pies cold for Sunday night supper with tomatoes and pickled onions. Besides being too heavy and meaty, they called up associations of Cam on Christmas night, complicated by jocular nautical allusions to Long Pig. He veered past the bacon as soon as he could move and fled up the next aisle, where he regained his composure among the cake mixes, which neither tempted nor distressed him. Two aisles farther on he found canned fruit and chose a jar of applesauce; applesauce was the last thing he could remember wanting more of, the last legitimate thing, at least.

Other shoppers looked at him oddly. Why did this man seem to be broken at the waist, Alan imagined them wondering. Why was his face such an unusual shade of pale green? They tended to swing wide around him in case he should go into whatever kind of spasm or fit he might be working up to. He did feel, himself, that he was fighting against time – could he finish shopping before he began retching? – but his stomach was so empty that he was not much concerned. Perhaps he could pretend to have a bad bronchial whoop. He was very grateful now that the place was no larger; he was halfway around.

After that, he acquired a tin of Carr's Table Water Biscuits on general principles, and some marinated artichoke hearts for Diana. The latter were a tiny pledge to himself that he'd go back, cured, and that she'd be waiting for him. When he saw meat give way to cheese he passed the back wall more slowly. As a cheese lover he felt ashamed as he passed up the Brie and Stilton for a packet of yellow plastic slices, but he would have to retrain himself to eat. In the next to the last aisle he strolled by a plump, unattended infant with only the tiniest of impulses to add it to the other groceries in his own cart. Coming in for the home stretch, past the bakery section, he picked up a package of butter tarts for whatever boost the sugar content might give him, though he expected trouble from outlaw raisins lurking in the silt at the bottom.

He had just paid and made it outside the store when his empty stomach began to flip, but he avoided being conspicuous (he hoped) by putting his head in the bag and pretending to examine the groceries closely and cough. The fresh air soon settled his stomach, and although he really was rather tottery now, he managed the trip back to his room without keeling over in the street.

Leaving his groceries casually in the bag, a proprietary finger-crossing to some touchy god of eating, he fished out a slice of cheese and nibbled it in little bites. Encouraged that the thing did not bite back, he unscrewed the top of the applesauce and swallowed a mouthful. Possible. He broke off a fragment of biscuit and nibbled it like the cheese. He began to feel full. His first bite of butter tart was an error, but he spat it into his handkerchief and was relieved to find the rest of his meal undisturbed. He lay down for safety's sake and fell asleep.

Three hours later, he awoke feeling hungry again, so he finished the biscuit with another slice of cheese and sat on the edge of his bed to think. It was afternoon now. What should he be doing? He recalled that people in his condition, or conditions vaguely like his but more normal, were supposed to eat small amounts frequently, which was what he seemed to want to do anyway. But could one spend one's time merely nibbling and napping? Apparently one could, for while he considered the issue he grew drowsy again and fell back on his pillow.

On his second morning in Toronto he awoke to find most of his cheese gone and his applesauce three inches lower. He had eaten at little intervals all night. He softened his orange by rolling it between his palms and sucked it. It tasted like breakfast. Coffee would have been good. After a couple of biscuits he changed his clothes and thought for a while. Then he removed the much abused pizza from his suitcase along with his spat-in handkerchief and dumped them into the supermarket bag with a shiver. He put on his jacket and set out in search of a trash can.

On his third day, when meals were more regular if still distinctly invalid in tone, he felt well enough to be bored. He felt ready for an expedition farther afield than the nearest supermarket or trash can. Yonge Street was still too rich for his blood. He was not ready to look up his friends, who really had been little more than acquaintances. He could hardly tell his supervisor why he had not been writing lately. And he was afraid to risk the university library. The thought of his supervisor, however, reminded him of a long-ago evening at the man's house in Rosedale, that elegant neighborhood. He remembered light coming through little mullioned windows to reveal the kinds of studies and living rooms that had furnished his fantasies of academic success ever since. A bus ride through Rosedale would be just the thing – passive, tranquil, inspiring.

He could get a bus from within the Rosedale subway station, he recalled, and he supposed he could just ride it in a circle without much objection. If not, he could pay another fare at the end of the line. But how was he to get inside the Rosedale station? Ordinarily he would just take the subway north at the Bloor/Yonge station, but the tumult and furor of that exchange even at a slack hour was such that the very thought of it made him want to lie down again. That, he told himself sternly, was no way to get better. If he could come down at Rosedale from the station above, he would be better off, but how could one get to Summerhill without the same problem?

In the end, feeling foolish and canny at once, he called a cab and rode to the Summerhill station in relative isolation, took the subway one stop, and got out amidst the shiny green tiles of Rosedale. Upstairs he found a bus already waiting under a sign that mysteriously said "Rosedale East und" but had to be right since the other said, God forbid, "Downtown." He slipped in the back door, no transfer being required, and sank into a single seat by the window.

As the bus turned right and rolled by the streets and houses of the prosperous, he knew that the ride would be all he'd hoped for. This was one of the Toronto faces that he loved best – brick houses of generous proportions, tiny parks with tall trees, squirrels. The old ladies who got on the bus as it passed through the tree-lined, hedge-bordered streets were wearing hats, not winter woollies but proper churchgoing sorts of hats. Clearly they always wore hats and gloves regardless of weather. The women who weren't wearing hats weren't speaking English either; he wasn't sure of the language, something like Portuguese maybe, but he suspected them of being maids or cleaning women. The old ladies probably called them charwomen.

Alan noted with appreciation some fancy stone walls on the left and an old gentleman walking two dogs. Children with their book satchels were running home. The black oxfords of their school uniforms were surpassingly ugly and their dark green knee socks were falling down, but they suggested a kind of unmistakable social stability. They fascinated him. For once he concentrated on substance and kept his fantasies in check, for he feared to arouse his distress about Diana by conjuring their Rosedalish future, and he was ashamed to think of attacking those very clean and wholesome youngsters on the sidewalk below (though the word homogenized did slip into his mind). The parents of those children had space for their marriages, rooms and whole floors to retreat to, complicated urban entanglements that would supply excuses for leaving the house.

The bus turned left onto Glen Road – the very name sounded green defiance of the bare trees – and on the far side of a rather fancy concrete bridge the houses got even fatter. And there was the little park he remembered. At the end of Douglas Drive a knot of borderline adolescents, boys of thirteen or so, were giggling together and watching for the bus out of the corners of their eyes. When it slowed down at the stop, one of their number, a sturdy blond boy whose every move sang of higher spirits than Alan could ever recall feeling, broke to the front of the group and flashed his overcoat open at the bus. He looked as though he were sharing the joke of the decade out of pure openheartedness. Could the child be exposing himself?

Alan leaned nearer the window and rubbed the condensation away with his fist. But how very long for a boy his age, how very pale and crooked. He started and banged his forehead on the glass, for it suddenly seemed to him that what protruded from the boy's unzipped trousers was the head and neck of a plucked chicken. Bad enough to have misperceived his own baby as an edible animal, but when it came to the private parts of totally unknown youths! He was giving himself up as hopeless when with a hoot of joy two of the other boys attacked the juvenile flasher and pulled from his pants an entire rubber chicken, which they waved about by its neck. Alan rubbed his head and snickered weakly with relief as the boys careened off down the street beside the bus, passing the bird like a football.

When he looked out again, the houses were shabbier and he was feeling worn at the edges himself. He barely enjoyed the stone dogs that he had overlooked on his way up as the bus completed its circle, and he thought of his bed with affection.

He should have been prepared, but wasn't, for the welter of hockey sticks, blazers, and nubile limbs rushing the bus back at the station. "Helen!" somebody shouted as he stepped off against the tide, and a thin, vivid, dark-haired girl on the edge of puberty swung around in his path and displayed a grin so wide and beguiling that he staggered. Or perhaps it was only the effect of his weak knees and the pressing, hot-blooded bodies. He fled north again, where he found a cab to carry him home.

Thus the third day. On the fourth and fifth days he consulted the papers and spent the afternoons in cinemas safely out of the downtown rush, watching films about modern urban situations with lots of traffic. He would come home quite incapable of remembering the plots, but a little less bushy and more blasé. On the second of these days, with a shaky affectation of casualness, he bought himself lunch (a plain omelet and coffee) in a small restaurant called Fran's. Nobody noticed him.

On the evening of the sixth day he sat down conscientiously to think about Diana, as he had heretofore managed to avoid doing. Evidently the public ramifications of his craziness were more or less over, but how about the heart of the thing?

He came to the pain first. It was not the relevant part, but he had to work it through. Why did she seem not to love, or even to like him, when he had done nothing outrageous? Of course he had been outrageous in his head, but she didn't know that, and her iciness had begun before his lunacy. Who would have thought that she could deal out such pain so steadily? How could it be that no customary device or ploy on his part did any good? Of course she was not behaving very badly; he knew marriages that would call cold silence a respite. But he also knew, as an anthropologist, that breaches, offenses against personal bonds, are a matter of context. In Mali, for instance, where best friends throw excrement at one another in greeting, a man is doubtlessly grieved at not being winged with a piece of flying crap when an erstwhile friends grows cool. He and Diana had been accustomed to talk, to bicker, to cuddle, to touch in passing. They had rejoiced in openness.

Suppose that this new icicled Diana was all the Diana he could expect in the future. Did he still love her? Still want her? A thousand times yes; better pain with her than bliss with someone else. So – Alan drew a long breath – here came the crux of the thing. *How* did he want her? Inside or out? Go ahead, he told himself, try a little cannibal fantasy. He gingerly imagined Diana's leg, her arm, her breast, and thought of biting each one. The idea aroused some excitement and a kind of unspecified longing. He still rather wanted to meld her into his body. His teeth still ground a little at the back molars. But, on the whole, he felt healthier than he had. He was not quite safe to be around yet, he judged, for he had brief flashes of blood lust in the midst of other reactions, but he was definitely better, maybe even marginally normal, given the wild nature of anyone's sexual fantasies. His steady desire to possess Diana had been distorted by a bad case of cabin fever, that was all. He was healing, and some day, possibly as soon as a week or so, he could go back.

CHAPTER SEVENTEEN

During the second week of his exile, when he was eating almost ordinary if somewhat bland meals and sleeping soundly, when his thoughts of Diana were approximately normal seventy-five to eighty percent of the time, Alan began trying to see his experience in some larger perspective. Though he had often enough tried to sort out the origins of his own difficulties, something occurred to him now that he had forgotten: he had not been the only peculiar thing in Wino Day. He thought with amazement of Naomi rousing herself to speak of eating Diana, of the men's babble about arctic spirits, of that mad proto-feminist Proxene Ratfat, whose ubiquitous scrawls made sense only to women. One might well, in such company, lose one's grip. He tried to recall whatever he had learned in his courses about cannibal superstitions. Almost nothing came back.

Perhaps it was time for his first excursion to the library. It would be good to find out more about the mass lunacy of the village and thereby, perhaps, to anatomize his own.

Despite his chronic tendency to fantasize, he had always believed that rational thought could exorcize anything and that rational thought was best stimulated by libraries. Nor was his conviction in the slightest degree weakened by any recollection (indeed, he had no recollection) of warm Toronto afternoons spent slack-jawed and catatonic, almost drooling, over his research in the university library while visions of Diana at home slunk through his head.

He had stayed away from the university until now for a number of reasons – fear of seeing someone he knew, fear of seeing no one he knew, fear of being trampled in the dither of academic busyness – but he loved the place and felt pleasurably excited at the thought of going there. His sense of pleasure grew as he walked past Trinity, past Massey, and watched the still newish library loom up, neck first, haughty as a stone peacock.

The scale of the thing, when he was actually at the doors, always made him feel about three inches high. He suspected the architect of having worked towards that effect; even so cathedrals (and sometimes government buildings) are designed to suggest super-human inhabitants. It had always made him snicker to imagine what the archaeologists of the future would make of Washington's outsize edifices, but he took the library seriously.

Inside, something struck him as wrong, or at least changed. He looked around. Everything seemed familiar – the speckled floor with its brass inlay, the elaborate coat-check mechanism, the escalators. He sat down on the steps a moment to rest and think about it.

He was the difference. The last time he had been here (ages ago it seemed, but he knew it must be less than nine months) he had been somebody else, a young, ambitious, happily married graduate student with a small baby. Young, especially. Smug, too. He had imagined that he had everything he wanted, or could get it. He had never watched an old lady die a grotesque death. He had never been on intimate terms with a disembowelled corpse. His thoughts had never constituted a major violation of human decency. The world had glittered all before him, or perhaps all around him, for he and Diana had been the center of it. Cam too. It came to him that he had once liked Cam rather more than he did now. Though not a lot.

The students who passed him looked remarkably callow. So, in some measure, did the professors. They hadn't been up there, up in Wino Day where things were hideously real, and they just didn't know. Down there either, he amended, considering the abyss of himself.

Feeling already more rational and razor-brained, he bravely stepped onto the escalator and soared up through the open central shaft to the card catalogue. He would look up "cannibalism" for starters. He reflected, as he pushed open the heavy doors to the reference area, that only a few days ago the colors of the carpet, exaggerated pea soup and tomato soup, would have seemed to him not merely ugly but nauseating. He was better, certainly.

"Cannibalism" offered surprisingly little. Perhaps it was not a popular topic here in the south. Louis Piton and his *Voyage à Cayenne* looked possibly useful, especially the fourth volume, but a publication by the American Ethnological Society seemed more urgent. The title gave him a premonitory twinge. *Windigo. Windigo Psychosis.* He made a careful note and hurried off in search of E99/A35/T4. The E's should be on the tenth floor. He half expected the fat Pakistani guard at the turnstile to turn him back for mental indecency – "windigo" had brought his guilt struggling back to the fore – but he passed through without incident and rode the elevator, twitching and jigging with nervousness.

Outside the elevator he hesitated, trying to recall the layout. He had spent a lot of time in this section once. He thought the yellow stacks on the right should do it. Or was it the red ones straight ahead? He chanced the yellow and found the book almost at once, a slightly outsized volume in a pale green paper cover. Stealing up to an empty table, he opened the pages nervously.

He skimmed the folk tales first, knowing they were the safer part, or if not exactly safe, at least more remote from himself. He'd face the section on psychosis later; would he find himself there? The stories ran from the poignant to the whimsical. He read about the gullible windigo who was greeted as "father" by a crafty woman who wished not to be eaten, about the weasel who was persuaded to crawl up the windigo's anus and bite the cord of his heart. Still, his knowledge that he was stalling made him uneasy, and unnerving phrases were beginning to jump off the pages at him:

> . . . and as winter came when they would be sleeping at night he'd bite the daughter and she would shout and they knew that he was going to eat her, so they killed him while he slept.

> . . . the monster tore out her entrails, and taking her body at one mouthful, started off without noticing the boy . . .

> The Windigo's wife was very glad that the Windigo was killed, for she was always afraid of him herself.

He moved on to the second part.

Two hours later, exhausted but relieved, he shakily put the book back on its shelf. He was convinced, despite some evidence to the contrary, that he had not been suffering from Windigo Psychosis. True, he had hungered after human flesh. True, he had been particularly inclined to attack his own family. Coincidentally, he had even seen his child as an edible beast, apparently a classic form of displacement colored by his own culture; Indians tend to see beaver or caribou instead of suckling pig. He had even behaved like the more honorable of the documented psychotics and fled lest he give way to his inappropriate desires.

Some other and rather major elements, however, did not fit. The premise that, given certain symptoms, people imagine themselves or their relatives to be turning into windigos because windigos are a familiar part of their mythic structure – that was a great relief. Back in Wino Day he had never for one moment believed any of old Mr. Benoani's ravings about windigos, nor had he taken seriously any talk of sinister spirits. He was not a man who believed that sort of thing, ever, at all, in his own culture or anyone else's. He was not susceptible.

His second point of relief was the heavily emotional and erotic content of his carnivorous desire for his wife. Though it was possible that any thought about Diana that he could produce would be in some measure emotional and erotic, the desires that had so gripped him did not feel like the ones the book talked about. That was fuzzily subjective, of course, not the voice of analytic reason at all. Still, he was convinced that the cannibals in the case histories had eaten their families out of convenience, not perversion.

He had simply let his damnable fantasies get out of control. He assessed his own character, not entirely with pleasure. He had always been an incurable fantasizer, dreamy and full of windy egotism. Had he ever been content with reality? Like a drowning man he was assaulted by pictures of himself from his babyhood on. He was lying in his crib, sitting on the front steps, sprawling in the grass, leaning on his school desk, sitting on his bedroom floor, loitering in the toilet, gazing at the ceiling, staring out the window, and dreaming, dreaming, dreaming. His block tower, long division, toothbrush, dinner, dissertation lay neglected before him. His real life ticked away as he laid waste his powers not only with imaginary getting and spending but, at various stages, with imaginary riding, shooting, swimming, flying, winning, fighting, fucking, courting, publishing, and flesh eating. If he had fantasized away four hours a day, probably a conservative estimate, and slept eight or more, then at least half his life had been spent in dreaming, not living. He was stunned. His life had been given over to Nothingness, a more icy and voracious creature than even the giant windigo.

Of all his mental debauches, his most recent had been much the most acute, rivalled only feebly by the weeks just after he had met Diana and by a period in his late childhood when he had aspired to membership in an exclusive gang of his elders. Would this condition of his get worse with age, until he was a prematurely doddering old loony? Or had the intensity of the last few weeks been brought about by peculiar circumstances, the isolation of Wino Day compounded by Diana's withdrawal and catalyzed by his accidental taste of human entrails?

In any case, he had to take himself more firmly in hand from now on. Good lord, no wonder Diana drew away from him. What had he given her to attach herself to? Character was going to be required of him. He hoped that he could work some up, unaccustomed as he was.

In a few more days, he decided as he reclaimed his coat and walked out into a slapping wind from the lake, he would arrange to go back home. He was surprised to hear himself think that word, but it was right – Diana and Cam equalled home. He need not be alone in his head, for he had a family to pull him outside, if he would let them. He would. He told himself that every time he had the slightest inclination to wool-gather, he'd snatch up his baby and bounce it on his knee until it did something so enchanting or obnoxious that he was brought back into focus.

He pushed his recovery substantially that night by taking himself out for dinner to a decent restaurant and having Beef Stroganoff. Meat was still very difficult for him, he discovered, even cut up into little strips and hidden in sauce. At one point he started to help it down by imagining that he was eating expendable scraps of his wife, but he caught himself after a few distressingly successful bites. If he couldn't do it right, he'd settle for eating noodles, dammit. More than one kind of recovery was needed, after all; the physical wasn't everything. He was embarrassed, but relapses, he told himself as he ate his salad, were human nature, and every day he felt more certain that the most ordinary of humans was what he wanted to be.

CHAPTER EIGHTEEN

The twenty-sixth of January, according to the travel agent, was the first day for which she could guarantee connections straight through to Wino Day Lake. Alan was a little disappointed, for having decided to go back, he would have liked to go back immediately. He knew, all the same, that a few extra days in town would do him no harm. He was not quite normal yet in his tastes and stability, and he could better repair his marriage if no part of his energy was going into the censoring of grisly inclination. Then too, he could buy some gifts as peace offerings, take his clothes to a laundromat, and generally get ready to present Diana with a new and improved husband. Now that he had stopped feeling frail, he was rather pleased to find himself slimmer. Maybe he'd even get himself something new to wear. There was still plenty of money in their Toronto account.

In pursuit of these resolutions, he set off on a cold, bright Thursday morning to shop his way to the Eaton Centre, starting at Bloor on purpose to make the expedition last. He still found Toronto weather mild after Wino Day and felt very healthy indeed as he strolled along, watching the other shoppers huddle in their collars. Pedestrian traffic was light. The shops looked pleasantly familiar. He smiled at the street distractedly and planned his next few days, interrupting his thoughts from time to time while he stopped to purchase a bit of Danish cheese here or a new paperback novel there. He would like Diana to know when he was coming back and be out there meeting the plane, but he suspected that a letter would not arrive in time. Of course, he could ask the Mounties to radio; they were always helpful to people in northern communities.

If he coped with the rush and sophistication of the Eaton Centre – and so far he felt quite a man of the world, not bushy at all – he would go on Saturday morning to the ultimate confrontation, the St. Lawrence Market. If he could survive that, not only the press of shoppers but the violent smells, the rows of internal organs and pendent carcasses, he would know himself cured beyond a doubt. And if he couldn't? Well, up to a point that wouldn't discourage him, for he had been a bit squeamish about it at his best. (Doctor, will I be able to play the violin? That's funny, I never could before.)

By the time he found himself outside the Centre, so aggressively modern, he had consolidated eight little packages and one dark blue chamois shirt into a shopping bag and was debating between perfume and a nightgown for Diana, who would surely be unable to resist his reformed state of mind and the effect of the moustache wax in his smallest package. Telling himself that the Centre was after all just a collection of shops like the ones he'd been in, only without the slush and automobiles, he made his way through the doors.

For a minute he almost ducked. Scores of wild geese were bearing down on him from above like a formation of bombers. He had forgotten that spacious hanging sculpture he had known and liked before. He could see that all the bush was not out of him yet; he hoped that the other shoppers had not noticed his flinch. The birds were splendid, though still subtly unnerving. He walked to the railing and admired them, trying to sort out his feelings. Something about them called up the quality of isolation of Wino Day.

His sense of well-being waned. He felt the back of his eyes sting. There had been the Christmas goose, of course, which he had nearly forgotten. But he thought that the goose recollection (which now made him abandon the notion of picking up some lunch while he shopped) was not the source of his difficulty. He suspected that the space around the geese contributed to his ambivalent homesick/sick-of-home feeling. That arched glass ceiling, didn't that bring back his old feeling of being trapped in a snoglobe? There was the sky beyond the geese, but they couldn't get to it. They were where they were, and they weren't going any place else. Maybe it was that, and their unlikeliness in the urban setting; zapped in mid-flight, they were isolated too. He shook his head and began to make the round of shops.

Maybe perfume *and* a nightgown. That would be safer. Every instinct shrieked and trumpeted for the nightgown, but he could perceive difficulties. For one thing, the whole topic of bed was pretty tricky. Bed, where they had made love and, even more awkwardly, where they hadn't. Where he had bitten her on the shoulder his last night in town. Out of where he had been ignominiously kicked. Further, Alan really preferred Diana to wear nothing at all to bed, though her custom varied by whim – nightgown, nakedness, tee shirt, and sometimes, when she was very very angry with him, all her clothes. Once her boots. He had gotten out and slept on the couch that time, suspecting that she intended, or hoped, to kick him in her sleep.

Would buying her a nightgown suggest consent to the end of nakedness?

And then there was the question of what sort of nightgown. Given the climate of Wino Day, voluminous flannel would be humane. It would show concern for her comfort at the expense of his own stimulation, possibly a good move. Certainly it would not suggest that he regarded her as a piece of meat – Oh shit, he said to himself, let's rephrase that – as a sex object, a prejudice of hers into which he had sometimes slammed and bruised himself.

On the other hand, visions of black lace danced a corny two-step in his head. Didn't all women secretly want to be overwhelmed sometimes with the sheer weight of ruffles? Mightn't there be in his cool Diana a residual child who had dreamed of grownup negligees and a full-scale knight to prostrate himself at her bedizened feet? Very likely, he told himself. Perhaps the rewinning of his erstwhile virgin goddess Diana, perpetually aloof of spirit, to his great frustration, lay in his luring her to a different and more properly feminine role, one of the lesser goddesses. Ceres, to make his bread. Hestia, to keep his hearth warm. Hestia would never need flannel; she'd be *his* cozy garment at night. The lacy nightgown would show that he understood the true, soft Diana inside. She'd love him more than she ever had.

After a full hour of careful shopping he found just the gown, gentle and frothy but vibrant. It cost him sixty dollars. And if Cam so much as dared lay a sticky finger on it, if Diana even thought about picking him up while she was wearing it – well, he wouldn't be responsible. He'd look into military schools for babies.

From then on he window-shopped idly, wondering whether he could endure lunch after all and feeling the richness of the free hours on his hands. He wouldn't begin to think about his dissertation again until he was

144

back in Wino Day and the domestic problems were cleared up.

He paused outside the Nag's Head to examine the sign and enjoy the potted plants. Half attracted, half repulsed by the odor of cooking food, he continued to idle, peering at the diners. His attention was caught and held by an elegantly suited middle-aged man with a white beard, man and beard both impeccable and slightly rounded. Loitering, Alan admired his air of urbanity and the genteel ecstasy with which he drained his beer. He wondered what the man had ordered. Something pretty sophisticated, he suspected, with that pinstriped weskit. He watched the waiter approach and set down a plate of sausages and potato. That was it? With astonishment he saw a rapture of anticipation sweep over the diner's face like the hush before a divine revelation. "Bangers and mash," the man breathed, and ordered another beer. Either, Alan told himself, he'd never really appreciated the holy mysteries of the dinner table, or he was spying on some kind of sausage pervert who would probably like to keep his climax to himself. He wished the elegant man well with all his heart and turned away lest he intrude upon the intimacy of the first bite.

As he went out past the geese again, he experienced another wave of uneasy feeling about Wino Day. It made him want to do something, but what? Maybe he'd go back to the library instead of going straight home. That windigo book was the only thing in Toronto that made Wino Day and his life there seem real, and he felt obscurely that it might answer some still unformulated question. He could grab a cheese sandwich and some coffee at one of the lunch trucks that ought still to be parked along St. George Street at this hour.

At the library he checked his packages with his coat, ignoring a glance from a Filipino attendant who looked as though she thought only faggots carried shopping bags, and hurried the escalator by walking up it. He felt a funny sense of urgency. On the tenth floor he made his way straight to the green paper-covered volume and sank into a chair outside the stacks, oblivious to the Chinese students just behind him who were soliciting cockroaches with their strictly forbidden lunches. He began again to skim from the beginning.

The first sentence of the introduction caught his attention for a moment. "What," it inquired rhetorically, "is the nature of the relationship between belief and behavior?" Alan thought it sounded like something he wanted to know and decided to keep an eye out at the end of the book for the answer. As he read, he began to see things he'd missed the first time. Or missed with his conscious, remembering mind; after all, he had been drawn back to the book for some reason. The symptoms of incipient windigo transformation were alarmingly familiar: even so had Naomi been without appetite, withdrawn, obsessed. Either her husband had read the book, or the book had been written from a lot of interviews with the old Mr. Benoanis of the Canadian north, for the writer certainly had the symptoms down pat. Northern Manitoba was one of the traditional places for Windigo Psychosis to flourish, too, though documentation suggested that the affliction was more commonly Cree than Chipewayan.

"The Windigo is not a sex-linked concept," he read in the folklore section, "since there may be either male or female windigos. However, they do not live together as married couples; on the contrary, each windigo is a solitary being." Alan was briefly amused by the dilemma of married windigos, each intent upon eating its immediate family. In a childless family, that could make for quite a battle of wills. He recalled a little engraving of two skeletons struggling in one another's grip; it had belonged to a witty friend of his who called it, "No, *I'm* the Dance of Death; You Come With Me." The same page supplied a rich profusion of variant terms for windigo: wintego, wetigo, wendago, wintigo, wintsigo, wiitiko, weendegoag, and so on. A rose by any other name, he told himself, still feeling determined to make light of the whole thing, though he was disturbed by the further information that the psychosis is likely to accompany a personality type that suppresses emotion, a description that seemed to fit most of Wino Day Lake's inhabitants.

Three case histories he found especially sobering. One, a detailed account of the Fiddler Trial, so much reminded Alan of the death of Naomi's great-grandmother that he wondered whether this could be her story. He supposed there was no way to find out now unless he asked Sarazine, whom he had been rather avoiding.

A second case, called "The Windigo Husband," made him grateful for Diana's own occasional suppression of emotion. It was a nasty little account of a woman who, suspecting her husband's inclinations, split his head open with an axe just to be on the safe side.

In the third account, a young man seduced into cannibalism by his wicked mother became terrifying to a cousin with whom he subsequently shared a bed, not only because he was feeling the cousin's ribs for fatness but because he smelled bad in an unspecified way, the sinister odor of cannibalism apparently analogous to the smell of any flesh-eater in the nostrils of less carnivorous cultures. That story brought back clearly a childhood nightmare, repetitive like the more recent Ratfat dreams and half a dozen in between. In it the child Alan, playing alone in his parents' house, would smell a sharp and unspeakably sinister odor and, panicking to find himself without adult protection, would wake up screaming. He had never understood that dream and he did not understand its resurrection now, but it worked on his nerves sufficiently to make him jump when a passing coed remarked to her companion, "There was blood on the door." Could the dream smell have been blood? Death? The girls whispered about him behind their hands as they moved away.

The cases went on and on, piling up disquieting detail. The world seemed full of windigos, a place where one's ankles might be snapped at by human teeth whenever one sat on a sofa. He pressed forward to the conclusion. What indeed *was* the relationship between belief and behavior? In a few more pages he found his unwelcome answer: so far as windigos are concerned, belief controls behavior utterly. It seemed then, that Naomi really might have eaten Diana, given strength and favorable circumstances. His view of her death changed a little; better to have institutionalized her than to have burst her vitals with hot tea, but better the hot tea than nothing. Diana was *his* wife. And while he was very glad not to have eaten her himself in a rash moment, he was damned if anybody was going to commit that kind of gastronomical rape in his stead.

Thumbing the last pages as an embryonic panic, not yet identifiable by species, revolved in the womb of his mind, he came to an appendix of windigo place names. So many of them! Did people always memorialize these ghastly incidents, and if so, what effect did names have on behavior? Windigo Falls and Islands and Lakes and Points and Rivers and Roads, with latitudes and longitudes, ran down the pages in tidy columns, reflecting what had doubtless been extremely untidy events. And what of the places that now wore aliases, one of which he had read about not ten minutes before – Brule Lake, also called Windego or Cannibal Lake in commemoration of an 1811 scandal? He sat up a little straighter in his chair, feeling his embryo flip over for birthing.

Where had he heard of a lake whose name was wrong on the map? Wine Dago Lake, not Wino Day! Wet Dago Lake, not about wet Dagoes after all! Wendago Lake,

Wetdigo Lake, that's what the natives had been saying so calmly. They knew what it meant, too, and went right damned well on suppressing their emotions!

He stood up with a wild gesture that provoked silvery oriental giggles from the rear, cold as bells. His hair prickled. He had left his wife, his child, all alone in that unholy place while he flew off to pamper his own nervous breakdown. He paced back and forth for a minute, blind with panic, his blood pressure singing in his ears. How could he get back to them fast enough? If those crazy natives did what they believed, and he knew that they believed in windigos, what was to prevent them from attacking an unprotected woman and child from another culture, another tribe, always fair game for cannibalism?

He tried to remind himself, as he dropped his book and propelled himself into the too-slow elevator, the snail-like escalator, that so far as he knew, nothing had happened in Wino Day and very well might not, that Willie would keep an eye on Diana, that this was the twentieth century. By the time he had run half way back to his room, simply because he needed to be running somewhere, his packages bumping against his leg, he felt less distraught. He was probably silly to be so frightened; why must he always swing to extremes? He slowed down and gulped the thin, cold air, thinking hard about the Bay store and galvanized buckets and second-rate films flickering on the Wino Day school projector on Saturday nights, safe and ordinary things incompatible with nightmare feasting. But he knew that until his arrival in Wino Day slowed his heartbeat to its normal pace, the days and nights would be indistinguishably long and dark.

CHAPTER NINETEEN

Gwyn River. Alan writhed in his hard, orange vinyl chair. He had been writhing in it for hours, getting up from time to time to re-ascertain that the coffee machine was broken. The battered old Ukrainian woman who had come in at one point to rearrange the dirt with a mop might have been Venus herself, so grateful was he to have something to watch besides the snow driving against the window. It had been dark for a while now.

After his last several days in Toronto, which hardly bore thinking about, he had stepped into the plane with the peculiar relief of a man finally going to meet the enemy. And this was the climax of all the panic and pacing, the nightmares and insomnia and nervous diarrhea, this godless, malicious, mother-freezing blizzard. Better, almost, to be without modern technology at all and to know oneself helpless than to be thus lured to false expectation. That he was not, at this very moment, on his way to Wino Day Lake was so contrary to his will that he was almost unable to take it in. Once, just for a moment, he had scared himself by not remembering where he really was.

What horror might be taking place in Wino Day right now, while he sat wingless in Gwyn River and glared at the parking lot? Did they come in the night, the human windigos? Break into the house like cat burglars and kill their sleeping victims? Did they knock at the door in the daytime and say they'd come for a cup of tea? Did they snarl and spring across the table, knocking the cups to the floor? Or perhaps they lay on their cots like Naomi until some kindly friend or relative bent over them to straighten their covers, and then they flung their arms around their benefactors' necks —

Who would it be, for Diana? Some neighbor woman? Willie himself? The family next door, all in an unlikely pack? Alan could imagine too vividly that heart-stopping moment when the windigo's nature declared itself and the familiar face shifted into ferocity. The hair at his collar prickled as he stared at his fellow passengers and pictured each face melting into something alien, eyes widening maniacally, lips drawing back from teeth.

Spooking himself wouldn't help the situation. He pulled his parka around him for comfort and examined the room for possibly the fiftieth time. Window onto airstrip. Orange and chrome. Grubby white tiles. Window onto parking lot. Not much of an inventory. A counter along one wall offered some visual relief, but it was thence that bad news issued. He had no grudge against Pacific West, which had managed to bring him in, but he contemplated the Calm Air sign with some bitterness. Calm Air. If it was so frigging calm, why weren't they going? Surely as a name it protested too much, especially juxtaposed to the bronze plaque commemorating dead bush pilots.

Oh to be a dead bush pilot, one's last fearful plunge all over. Compared to that, being a live Alan hadn't much to recommend it. If he found Diana safe, though, and Cam of course, then life might be worth it, at least if she was safe and glad to see him as well. But all that was in the problematic future, which felt as though it might never come. Perhaps the snow would go on and on until the air terminal was preserved under five hundred feet of it, and someday diggers would find his bones frozen in the posture of waiting, like bodies baked in action at Pompeii. He felt already as if the diggers were long overdue.

There would have been some perverse comfort in keeping vigil in the terminal all night; it would have felt like trying to get home. But heartless officials had announced that they'd be locking the terminal as soon as they heard from the last flight scheduled in. He would be obliged to take a cab into town and spend another sleepless night in another strange bed.

The wide main street, as he stepped out of his cab with his suitcase and faced the snow-laden wind, was as bleak as he'd known it would be. The ends of the earth, after Toronto, without being home. Siberia must be like this, he thought. What was so peculiarly bleak and mean about small towns in the north, as though, like the vegetation, they had been stunted by too short a growing season? Not many buildings even grew to two stories; their skins were drab and lustreless, their glass dull. Half the meagre shops were shut already, and the others could not conceivably have anything he wanted.

The street, however, was in some ways preferable to the emptiness of his room (thirty-six dollars a night in the segregated white annex over the hardware store). The Indians at least had a bar in their hotel instead of a window full of axes and tea kettles. Alan left his suitcase by the bed and wandered back out, killing time until he could lie down for another white night. It wouldn't take long to window shop the blighted stores of the one main street. He loitered by the dim panes of glass, stopping to lean against the jewelry store and play a variation of a private childhood magazine game – which one thing on this page would I choose to own? Now he imagined which object in the window he could with least offence bring to Diana. Given the choices available, his game provided a welcome intellectual challenge. Besides, the thought of buying her gifts made Diana seem illogically safer. You don't buy jewelry for a pile of picked bones, right? Nobody ever says, "I'm so sorry but I'd like to return this brooch because the neighbors have eaten my wife."

Not the fake turquoise. Not the crosses. Not the praying hands or zodiac keyrings. Certainly not the china doggies. How tacky everything was! He wiped his frosty breath off the window with his sleeve and tried to look more closely at the ring tray. Diana didn't wear rings very much, but there was some limit to how ugly a ring could be. Just as his nostrils began to ice together, he settled on an almost plain gold ring with a square onyx stone. Its design was decently chaste but not too masculine. It would look good on Diana's long fingers. Maybe he'd even get it tomorrow if the store was open before he left, and if he had enough money.

The night was too cold and the game too unprofitable to window shop very long. What were his options? He could go back to the room and try to read. He could blot out a couple of hours in the local movie theatre. He wandered to the other end of the street to read the billboard. They were showing *Attack of the Killer Tomatoes*. The photographs suggested that it might be the worst film Alan had ever had a chance to see. Ordinarily he would have found that irresistible (more so if Diana had been laughing beside him and sharing a box of popcorn), but he felt a little ill at the attack of killer anythings just at the moment. Not impossible for a man who had only a few weeks ago cringed at the sight of food to imagine tomatoes as sinister. Unbidden rose the image of their ankle-snaring vines, their monstrous globulosity, their obscene and gelatinous guts. No, he would not see the film.

Instead, and why had he not thought of it earlier, he would go into one of the bars and drink himself into a mild stupor. He would sleep after all. Which would it be, the Canadian Legion bar, or the Crazy Horse, the Indian bar in the hotel? He felt shy of Indians at the moment in much the same way that he felt shy of killer tomatoes, but at the steps leading down to the Legion bar he remembered other Legion bars and hesitated – the austerity, the suspicious glances at his hair and moustache from burly bare-scalped men who could beat him into jelly, from hefty women in stretch pants who might consider driving their spiky heels into his gut for the sake of their children. Though, in truth, no attack had yet been actually launched on him in a Legion bar, even an American one.

He would go to the Crazy Horse. Was he an anthropologist or not? The Indians would let him alone. He could watch and get drunk and be all right. He crossed the street again and found his way to the Indian hotel. How could a place so close have the aura of a subtly less desirable neighborhood? The trampled snow still held suggestions of last night's congealed jetsam, and happy, rowdy noises issued from somewhere behind the aluminum storm door. They grew in volume as Alan crossed the vestibule and pushed through another set of doors, brown and wooden. Now this was a bar! It reminded him a little of his undergraduate days. The air was smoky, the voices raucous. A mirrored sphere revolved in cheerful vulgarity from the ceiling. He saw two or three other whites from the plane and caused no stir as he found his way to an unoccupied booth.

By the time his second beer sat in front of him, he was feeling better. The place was warm, and the din wrapped itself around him like cotton wool. He was beginning to like the music, chiefly loud songs of lust and truckdriving. He was alone without having to be by himself. Of course he was still so knotted with tension that he felt like a piece of bad macramé, and his need for Diana was borderline hysterical, but he could hold out for a while. If he held himself very rigid. If he imagined that she was only off in the ladies' room. The divorce songs were not so good. He made the wet ring from his glass into a capital D and rubbed it out with his fist, feeling silly. But he had not looked at it long enough, so he wet his finger on the side of his glass and made a more furtive one inside the sheltering crook of his left arm.

He would never let Diana out of his sight again. The crash of music around him was too feeble to express the decibel level of desire shouting in his blood. He would go back and feed off Diana's sweetness for the rest of his life. She had to be safe for him to come home to, she just had to. His craziness had been after all merely a nervous and misguided manifestation of his great need of her nourishing presence. He hadn't wanted to share her with Cam when he needed the extra rations for his writing. Certainly she was the source of all goodness for him, and if his world, Diana, was now in her winter cycle, it must follow that spring would come. He began to suspect that he was a little drunk.

Something, he realized, had been happening while he was lost in amorous metaphor. Everyone was watching the dance floor.

"Who's that?" he asked his nearest neighbor. "What's going on?"

"Old woman from Pukatagosis," his neighbor said tersely. He threw a quarter out onto the floor with an accustomed flip.

Alan watched a short, broad woman in a purple satin jacket, her grey hair stringing out from a kerchief, squat to gather up coins and then make for the bar. Her throat, her waist, her arms were hung with transparent scarves like the bows on a French Christmas tree.

"Why does everyone pay for her beer?" Alan wanted to know.

"Might as well. She drinks yours, you don't watch it," his new friend said, and offered him a joint. It *was* like college. "She drink anybody's."

The old woman's wide face above the dirty white frills of her blouse, expressionless even for a native (expressionless for a turnip, come to that), seemed in its triumphant witlessness almost to lack features beyond the brown bottle plugged into its lower portion. It was as close to a tabula rasa as Alan ever remembered seeing. He was grateful for this new distraction.

The old lady from Pukatagosis abandoned her empty bottle and moved back onto the dance floor, sizing up the couples. This was definitely more fun than killer tomatoes. She settled on a couple in their thirties, the man paunchy but aggressively youthful, the woman almost as decorated as the old lady herself. A murmur of anticipation swept the drinkers. Old Lady Puck, as Alan thought of her, stood hand on hip behind the man, watching his steps, nodding to herself. Moving in closer, very close indeed, she began to dance, aping his gestures. Alan had never supposed that one human being could stay so close to another without touching. Old Lady Puck kept her drunken balance and never made a false move; she had absorbed the dancer's system. Clearly, from the response of the regulars, she was known for this.

The man she danced behind began to sweat about the temples. He knew himself ludicrous but pride demanded he stay on the floor and ignore her until the dance was over. Alan had never seen anything quite like it. The old woman was only a head or so above the dancer's waist. She looked like a fleshy bustle, or some kind of fat, complicated tail. Her echo of his steps was exquisitely mocking, her inscrutability absolute. It was somehow the repetition itself that pointed up the absurdity of the man and his dance, as a jest twice told may reveal its asininity. The dancer's by now dispirited thrusting of pelvis and bending of knee were caught up and ridiculed in Old Lady Puck's pudgy hopping. Not a man in the room but felt a kindred embarrassment and thanked his gods that he had escaped personal exposure.

"Proxene Ratfat in fancy dress," Alan mused beerily. "Proxene Cityrat." But the thought of Proxene had been a mistake. All his anxiety about Diana pounced again with a new embellishment – Proxene lurking in the shadows to see the dreadful feasting. He could see her all too clearly, crouching at the edge of the light like a jackal. Did windigos share with the poor like regular villagers? Would Proxene be thrown a foot or a bit of neck?

If Alan's neighbors at the bar were surprised to see him leap up with a strangled sob and bolt for the door, they didn't think about it long. White people act funny in the winter.

CHAPTER TWENTY

Wino Day lay black beneath them. Alan's spine ached from the last fifty minutes of wanting to sit on the edge of his seat in a plane that was almost too small for short people sitting well back and relaxed. Other bits of him ached as well – his jaws, from the nervous grinding of his teeth, his stomach from anxiety. He pressed his forehead to the curved wall near his share of the window and tried to see something. The shell of the Otter thrummed and vibrated against his frontal bone. He could tell that they were beginning to dip down, but he couldn't see any houses. Shouldn't he have seen lighted windows by now? Had a giant windigo come and swallowed up the entire village? Well, the pilot acted at any rate as though *he* could see something, so perhaps it was all right.

Would Diana be there to meet him? Would she have missed him, forgotten her hostility, hug and kiss him hello? She would be cushiony in her parka and smell like soap. They would go home together in the cold to their warm house, and he'd unpack the black nightgown and the artichoke hearts and the other things, and tonight he wouldn't have to sleep twelve inches away. He was wearing his new shirt. His moustache was waxed at the ends. He'd taken a shower before he left Gwyn River. O please let her be there and love me, he besought some unspecified power, or at least like me all right, want me.

If she wasn't there he'd just walk home from the airstrip with his suitcase and fling open their door and she'd run to meet him. But if she was so all-fired glad to see him, why wouldn't she have come to the airstrip? She'd say she hadn't wanted to leave Cam. Alan's temper rose a little at the thought of it. And he'd say, "Why couldn't you have gotten someone to stay with him?" And she'd say, "Because he loves his own mother best." And *he'd* say, "Well he's had you all to himself while I've been away; what about me?" And she'd say, "You're old enough to take care of yourself, I should think," and her tone would be lofty and sarcastic. Then he'd throw his suitcase – no, he'd take it and march off to Willie's house and go away again the next day; she made him so fucking mad with her mindless babying of Cam that he didn't care if he never saw her.

Alan turned off the dialogue with an effort. He was falling into a real rage from a hypothetical quarrel. Of course he loved her. Of course he was going to stay, no matter what.

He could see some kind of queer illumination now. It looked like snowmobile headlights. The generator was out, then. He had heard of this happening once before, the snowmobiles all going out and lighting up the airstrip so the plane could land. Diana would surely be there in that case, if she was all right. Likely the whole town would be out to see the excitement, and nobody would want to sit home in the dark. They were getting very close to landing now. He could see shadowy forms mounted on the snowmobiles, and a sparse, hard snow driving aslant of the lights.

Their approach was somehow disconcerting, eerie as though they were coming in from an impossible angle or as though the lights outlined a vertical doorway into darkness. He scanned the crowd but couldn't see anyone with Diana's posture or clothing, or, as they came closer yet, her face; but he lost sight of the crowd as they touched down and bumped to a stop, so perhaps he'd just overlooked her. His stomach knotted.

He took his suitcase and packages and hurried down the steps, missing the last one and jolting onto the packed snow. He cast a wild eye around him. No Diana. Was she okay? People were avoiding his eyes, weren't they? Weren't they? He ran at the crowd, which seemed to melt away from his advance. Dropping and recovering his bundles, he managed at last to catch Willie's reluctant sleeve.

"Have you seen Diana? How is she?" he babbled. "Is she okay? Why didn't she come?" He wondered remotely even as he said it if Willie himself might not have eaten her, in which case she was as close to him right now as she'd ever be again. But that, he knew, was really craziness, and he had to trust someone. Couldn't that damned impassive Indian see that he was mad with anxiety? One tear eased out onto his right cheek and froze.

Willie's glance, kind but very guarded, flicked over him for a moment before it shifted away and he shrugged. "Go find out," he said finally. "You take my flashlight. Little trouble maybe."

Alan snatched it and ran, panic mounting in the back of his throat. With the flashlight he could see just enough to keep on the airstrip road. It was very hard to tell how far he was getting. He was simply running in a huge black waste, hurrying, perhaps, to a piece of bad news that would make his life turn a corner, poison his whole past and cripple his future. Still, Willie would have told him if Diana was dead, wouldn't he? She must be alive, mustn't she? Reason, alas, penetrates only the mind's outer layer and never gets anywhere near the knees or the pit of the stomach. He felt not at all reassured, and snow was beginning to sift down his collar. His feet pounded heavily down (lit-tle trou-ble may-be) and each jolt seemed to travel upwards and sink footprints in his own breast. Even before the cold turned his breath to razor blades and slowed his pace, he had the sensation of being in a nightmare where he was running through molasses. He could hardly remember whether he was running *to* or *from.* "Slower than molasses running uphill in January," his mother used to say when he dawdled. Slower than molasses in Wino Day.

His mind had never been so empty. All his seething, busy little dreams had retreated into the far convolutions of his brain to make room for the big thing coming. Vacant lifetimes, dynasties, epochs elapsed before he suddenly recognized the back of a house just two away from his own. He slowed again, fearful of revelation, and at last approached his trailer with stealth, stalking the bad news so it wouldn't see him. The windows were altogether dark.

Alan stood in front of his door and got his breath. His flashlight beam gleamed on the metal. The door held back its secrets like a coffin lid; what horror might not be rotting behind it? He swept his beam back and forth on the ground, looking for some clue as to what he would find inside the house. The marks of many feet? Blood? Torn clothing? Diana's own little reassuring path, coming in and out from the post office or the store?

Smooth and unmarked, broken only by dry grass near the steps, the snow lay along the front of the trailer, sparkling a little in the sudden light. The apparent lack of activity was puzzling. He felt better at the evidence that nobody had gone in. (Unless they had ways to cover their tracks? Which, come to think of it, seemed pretty likely.) But why had Diana not come out? Was she dead? Imprisoned? Or merely – he seized on it almost with delight –

very ill? That was a new idea. He'd had his mind on the mental illness of his neighbors. But the neighbors ought to be helping her, if she was ill. He wondered briefly why nobody else was back from the airstrip yet. He might be the last man on earth.

Could Willie have meant illness when he referred to "trouble"? Of course it might even be Cam's illness. Please, he thought, let it be Cam's trouble. Though he always disliked Diana's having to nurse him.

If Diana herself were ill she *would* be glad to see him. For a moment the weight on his mind lifted as he saw himself, clean and strong in his new blue shirt, magnanimously hovering over the bed of this woman who'd been so cold to him when he left. The specifics (hot soup? cold cloths?) were foggy because he didn't know what she had, but the picture was pretty.

Impelled by a rush of solicitude, he put his hand to the door and found it unlocked. She might have gone to bed early. Alan kept the beam of Willie's flashlight directed near his feet; he had been touchy about falling since Christmas night. The house was black around him.

He stared at the pattern on the kitchen linoleum and shivered, though the room seemed much too hot. The air was close, stifling, and it didn't smell of the Diana he knew. Alan felt the hair shift on the back of his neck and along his arms.

"Diana?" he asked into the silence. "Honey?" He almost jumped at the sound of his own voice.

"It's me," he whispered, because he had meant to say it but suddenly didn't want to make a noise.

His wife's voice came from the far side of the kitchen, cool and mocking as an echo: "It's me."

Swinging the beam up from the floor, he saw that she was sitting at the table naked. How very odd, and it didn't seem like a welcoming gesture designed for him, for she hadn't combed her hair, perhaps not for a long time, and her expression – well, "self-contained" hardly touched it, and "haughty" was too out-going. He edged his way to the table and perched a tentative haunch on its corner. The flashlight, laid on the oilcloth, illuminated her left breast and cast a half-light on her inscrutable lower face. Alan steamed under his parka. He'd have liked to take off some clothes, but this didn't seem the time. Diana's breast floated white against the darkness. He felt his penis fatten sluggishly in its sweaty bed and subside again as he leaned closer. He could hear the clock tick in the bedroom.

"Well I *am* glad to see you," he said. "As much as I can see you, of course, in the dark like this." He wagged his flashlight playfully and rather wished he hadn't, for the shadows still sprang like beasts. "I guess I owe you some kind of apology for acting so crazy before I left," he yammered, "but I've got my head together now and we'll be all right."

He gazed at the flat, black window, where he could almost see a ghost of himself, giving Diana her chance to say that she guessed she needed to apologize too, and rehearsing his generous response. That transaction over, things would begin to be right. He liked the darkness less than ever. Why didn't Diana answer? He had to remind himself that it was indeed her face across from him, that he'd seen it clearly. Even the innocent phrase "her face" was unsettling, suggesting as it did a face owned by Diana, in which he had no share. To comfort himself, he moved the light a little, so that he could see both breasts.

Leaning forward cautiously, he caught her scent. That too held him at bay. Where was her perfume, her soap? Indeed, he began to suspect that she had not known soap for some time, that it had been abandoned with her comb. She smelled sharp, sweaty, secret, and, in some elusive way, alien.

He wet his lips and managed to ask, "You all right?" "*Are*

you?" he urged when she didn't answer. In the shadows she seemed to ape his gesture.

Alan wanted to reach out but dreaded to touch her. He flexed his hand by his side and delayed. At last he pushed his fingers through the thick air and laid them on her forehead before she drew back. He would not have been surprised to scorch his hand on her skin, but her forehead was cool as snow, despite a trickle of sweat down her throat.

He began to gabble again. "Don't you think we ought to turn the heat down, of course you're not wearing anything, are you, but you could put your robe on, is it clean? We should have some candles somewhere, no need to sit in the dark, and you can't see what I've brought, can you, like this? Are you sure you're not sick? How's Cam?"

He stopped short at the sound of the last question. How, indeed, was Cam? Shouldn't he be up and yelling at the sound of his father's voice? Had this woman, this mad wife from a Victorian attic, been taking care of his son? He swung the light up to look into those eyes that had been watching him in their darkness all along, and urged the question in a new form.

"*Where* is Cam?" he said distinctly.

The change from gabble seemed to catch Diana's attention. "Gone," she said indifferently. Then a jaunty and feral grin animated her face and she added, " – almost." She gestured to the counter in the darkness at her left.

Dying, did she mean? Was his little body expiring on the counter or what in hell was going on? Alan stumbled over his suitcase and flashed his light along the wall, dreading to look. Only mouldy dishes and clutter met his gaze, and one fresher platter with a little mess of underdone stew in the middle. Reluctantly he poked at the soggy mass with the tip of his – finger? Little bones, joined together, like. Like. Fingers? A pudgy little hand? *Cam?*

He felt, to his surprise, a wave of real grief for his boy, fellow-feeling for a lover whose source of nourishment had turned against him. With no intellectual pleasure he perceived the symmetry of the feeder becoming food, nor did he envy Cam the intimacy of being back in Diana's body. Still, he struggled to ally himself to the woman whom he had adored so hard and so clumsily for so long, to believe that she was recoverable, that she was merely having a breakdown. With her susceptibility to new ideas, the windigo myth had been too much for her and she'd gotten hungry for Cam – he knew how that felt – and now she was coming apart from the stress. And he had been too selfish to notice what should have been obvious.

They would have to account for the baby's loss, of course; there would be trouble. He'd make himself an accomplice. She could plead insanity. Perhaps they both could. Or maybe they could just go some place new, if Diana got better, and never tell. "What baby?" they would say to his parents, or invent some story later, crib death perhaps. The Indians would be unlikely to tell the Mounties; that was not the way their heads worked. He and Diana would become part of their mythology: there was once a white man and his wife who came for a winter and were taken by the spirit of the windigo; they ate their child and went away to their own land.

And he and Diana would be hiding in the States and sharing this secret they'd never speak of, which would bind her to him forever. He would renounce the claims of fatherhood and share her guilt. He entertained suddenly a sick desire for Diana even as she was at that moment, a yen to roll and tangle with her unwashed body as well as join her in moral corruption. He started to wipe his fingers on his pants but defiantly sucked them clean instead.

As if in response to his thought, he heard her chair scrape back and the pad of bare feet on the floor. He turned to her, keeping the beam of the flashlight down.

Better to consummate this final union in a dark, steamy dream. He held out his arms, remembering how it felt to want her inside him, and pulled her against the length of his body. Her left hand slipped under his parka and played over his ribs, and although her body stayed rigid, she pressed herself against him. Her smell would certainly need a little getting used to; he hadn't realized how much he had identified artificial scents as hers, as her in fact. Crushing her closer, he hung his chin over her shoulder and nuzzled her neck. "Diana," he moaned, and then he saw his hunting knife, bright in the beam of his flashlight.

"I've been waiting for you," she murmured, speaking for the first time the words he had longed to hear, and drew her right hand out from behind her back. Time stopped as his mind protested at the wrongness of it – no, no, this was not fair. He did not want them to be one if it meant her absorption of him. This was not what he'd intended, not at all! This was not love, not romance, it was pain and gastric juices and an ignominious end in the intestines – too intimate by half.

Unbidden, not his choice for a last fantasy, came a vision of his death à la Ratfat: two small human figures (one very small indeed) sucked into a monstrous, fang-fringed orifice. Would she really draw that, he wondered briefly, and whose kitchen wall would it disfigure? And then he felt the first big tooth catch in his backbone.

Also of interest

WOMEN FLY WHEN MEN AREN'T WATCHING
Sara Maitland

For twenty years Sara Maitland, one of Britain's most acclaimed writers, has chronicled the imaginative and actual concerns of women's lives shaped by feminism in a series of stunning short stories and novels. The breadth of her interests and inspiration are brilliantly displayed in this gathering of tales old and new: from folk-stories in 'True North' to classical mythology in 'Cassandra'; from historical incident in 'Forceps Delivery' to Christian heroines like Perpetua in 'Requiem'. And as she intertwines the everyday and the inexplicable to witty or disquieting effect in 'Greed' and 'The Loveliness of the Long Distance Runner', her wildest flights of fantasy remain anchored in a consciousness of the oppression of women, overlaid with a wickedly ironic humour.

AQUAMARINE
Carol Anshaw

**'*Aquamarine* is as dazzling as the gemstone, as cool as deep water. Carol Anshaw has both flash and substance'
– *Rita Mae Brown***

With striking ingenuity, *Aquamarine* explores the intricate ways early choices, made impulsively or agonizingly, reverberate throughout a life. Jesse Austin, on the verge of turning forty in 1990, is inhabiting three equally plausible lives: married, pregnant, living in her home town of New Jerusalem, Missouri and having an illicit affair with a maverick skywriter almost half her age; lesbian English professor in New York bringing her lover back to Missouri on a visit; divorced mother of two, running a down-and-out swimming academy in Venus Beach, Florida. Each is haunted by the moment she can't get back to, the moment hidden behind the aquamarine, when she lost the gold medal for the hundred-metre free-style at the 1968 Olympics to a fatally seductive Australian swimmer named Marty Finch.

With wit and wry affection, Carol Anshaw explores the unlived lives running parallel to the ones we have chosen.

COWBOYS ARE MY WEAKNESS
Pam Houston

**'Pam Houston has verve and perfect pitch . . . she snaps
along in a sassy canter, her prose sharp and clean'**
– New York Times Book Review

Sharp, touching and often hilarious, this stinging-fresh collection
of short stories, from a powerful new voice, will open up new
worlds of high deserts and Alaskan tundra, of perilous white
water and frozen rockies. Pam Houston's women – part
daredevil, part philosopher – know they should know better, but
they don't: they wrestle within themselves, with danger, and
above all, with their men (whose bodies speak volumes but
whose emotions are not so communicative). Sexy, gutsy and
intoxicating these twelve tantalising tales are written in spare,
exhilarating prose.